A Novel ~

CHRIS WILSON

THE HARVESTER PRESS

A Harvester Novel
First published in Great Britain in 1987 by
THE HARVESTER PRESS LIMITED
Publisher: John Spiers
16 Ship Street, Brighton, Sussex

© Chris Wilson, 1987

British Library Cataloguing in Publication Data

Wilson, Chris
  Baa.
  I. Title
  823'.914 [F]   PR6073.I439/

  ISBN 0-7108-1230-2

Typeset in Palantino 11 point by
GCS, Leighton Buzzard, Beds
Printed in Great Britain by Billings & Sons Ltd, Worcester

THE HARVESTER PRESS PUBLISHING GROUP
The Harvester Group comprises The Harvester Press Limited
(chiefly publishing literature, fiction, women's studies, philosophy, psychology, history and science and trade books), and
Wheatsheaf Books Limited (chiefly publishing economics,
international politics, women's studies, sociology, and related
social sciences).

To Saara, Hannah and William

The glacier knocks in the cupboard,
    The desert sighs in the bed,
And the crack in the tea-cup opens
    A lane to the land of the dead.

W. H. Auden

This is a fiction, innocent of any historical, geographical or scientific truth.

Every word has been fully processed.

Texturised and reconstituted meanings, acetic acid E260, stabiliser E412, flavourings, colour E172, preservative E223, antioxidant E320.

Contents

Aakmaa's Quietner

3 Ludwig Prospect
Helikfors,
1st June 1891

I, Count Doctor Friedryk Baa MindeBerg, natural scientist, Royal Academician, Chairman of the Committee of the Institute of Geography, have a confession to make. On the creamy skin of these pristine pages I lay my fat black slug of a secret to trail its mucused path.

Passing through nature, I once ate a man.

There! I have written it down. It is no slight thing to have been compelled by hunger to ingest another's person.

This tincture—Aakmaa's Quietner—is a six per cent solution of opium in alcohol, flavoured with oil of anise and coloured with Priinski's Purple. It is prescribed for the relief of toothache. My teeth are sound and wholesome. Sadly, I have no pain on which to deploy and test it. Furthermore, it strikes me as an effete and uninteresting solution. Having now dosed myself with a single, then double, then quadruple dose, I discern but the mildest sedation. Yet there are cosmetic effects. The tincture colours the mouth deep purple. There are also blotchy stains to a man's hands, and to the lap of my trousers where I inadvertently spilled it.

I often think of him. A man cannot exaggerate the pains and regrets that dog him through the years when he has been compelled to consume a friend, fellow traveller and member of Bryke's Club. Tinging this compound sadness is

1

a shock of impropriety. He who had been meat and drink to me for full thirteen days had been the Captain of my School. Indeed, in my junior year I had fagged for him. Though he was a harsh task-master, he often gave me a muffin. How our positions change in this bagatelle of life!

He was large-boned, fatty, slack-muscled, sinewy and obstinately gristled. As we ate him—Bertii Smugsen and I—we could not help but note and lament the physical decline in him since he had led us to the Feetball Cup in '57 and '58. We ate first the most obvious and prepossessing portions of his person, but after eight days were forced to nibble his bony extremities. Though we had taken care to smoke him well, he grew quite rancid, clinging with a cloying sweetness to the palate. I recall him clearly now, across all these years of separation, in the various forms of our association—as boy, School Captain, man, colleague, friend and taste. To this day, if I can avoid offence to my host, I decline pork out of repect for my lost companion.

I have never spoken or written of this before. There is decorum to be considered; and the feelings of his relatives. I hazard to suppose they should prefer him buried the hero in a shallow, sandy grave in Chimba than eaten by a Fellow of the Institute of Geography.

Smugsen passed on also, as we neared the safety of Baa MindeBerg Junction. So the secret lies snug with me. In my account of the expedition (*Journey to the Interior*, Aalberg and Brygstaadt, 1st edition, sixteen ffenyngs) I bequeathed to both the pretty fictions of more honourable ends than they gained for themselves. Oistermaa, I wrote, had been speared in an ambush, bravely fighting for his comrades. Smugsen, whom I liked the less, I had succumb to the persuasions of cholera.

Some load is lifted just to write of this, yet replaced by some other. I feel suffused by serenity. Its colour is radiant amber. It has the tangibility of some translucent mass stretching beyond my sight, smothering me with the weight of mountains, yet fondling me in its crush. I digress.

Bertii Smugsen and I ate Oistermaa—even the name speaks his solidity—on the Chimba trail in '66. Having been at Naval School together, and trusting each other as decent enough fellows, as Navalists can, we had pooled our provisions, mules, guides and bearers to push up through Chimba Gap. This gorge is approached indirectly, along two arms of an L, for a range of mountains discourage the direct route. We expected perils, though not those we met. It is a harsh, parched, desolate path in the dry season. The ground is ochre sand, speckled by flints. All vegetation dies back to lie dormant as grits of seed, placing faith in distant rains. Animal life is of insects and reptilians, save for occasional birds of prey which sore and circle, swooping only for a scurrying beetle, the maimed or dead.

This land holds the burial grounds of the !Tng tribe. In this was further difficulty. Our Kymbi bearers disdain yet fear the !Tng. They explain that the !Tng eat locust, couple with rhinoceroses and display unkindly temperaments. The !Tng, in turn, have historical complaints. They say that the Kymbi angered their rain god by stealing his foreskin. There is no love lost.

So as we trudge towards the !Tng lands, broiled by unrelenting sun, our bearers become awkward, dispirited and fearful. They tell us there is nothing along this path but sand like that we walked upon. We explain we act the eyes for a great King, and must needs look wheresoever he has instructed us. The next day, they seek to discourage us with a different tale—that the world ends along this route in a bottomless chasm. We profess great interest in seeing this hole. This angers them further.

On the third night of our journey, whilst we three sleep, huddled together for security, the best portion of our bearers decamp, taking a disproportional share of beasts and provisions. We are thus compelled to order those that remain to flog each other for not restraining those that have left. This is in accord with local custom, as with the rules of Ponsfors Naval School, that each take responsibility for all and be accountable for their conduct. The

3

beatings, as those at school, though harsh are fair. For we have taken care to appoint only the most decent and reliable of the tribe to the rank of Full Prefect. But the disipline proves counterproductive. The next night, the remainder of the train depart with all the remaining goods and beasts.

This would have been vexing enough, but before leaving, they have stripped us of clothes and bound us together. At least they leave us our lives. Like schoolboys, they might debag an unpopular master, but gag at cutting his throat.

We make ourselves busy the rest of that day trying to free ourselves from our tight naked conclave. Having finally effected our release, we are rubbed quite raw around wrists and ankles—where the thongs had bound us—are scarlet from sunburn, considerably hungry and rapaciously thirsty.

Lizards are neither appetising nor easy to catch. They seem lethargic enough, basking upon stone. Yet when approached as supper they flit away to dissolve in sand. I have the good fortune to detain one by the tail. But I am left clutching just that—a dry, scabrous column of bone. I pass it around to share with the others. We chew upon it in turn. Each agrees it provides little enough satisfaction.

Having no food, water, clothes or transport, and being at almost a week's walk from base, surrounded by sands in which each direction presents an identical, mocking hostile face, we naturally worry for our welfare. Dehydration, sun-stroke and hunger blunt our movements, shorten our tempers and slow our progress. Misfortune marries disaster and breeds catastrophe. We follow the wrong path for two days.

Being a practical man, and not prone to false sentiment, I see before the others the lamentable course to which two of us must needs resort, and the third will acquiesce. We have a practical problem demanding practical solution, governed by practical logic. I see too, without self-interest, that, as a slight and short man I cannot nourish the others for long.

If the lives of three young gentlemen be of equal value, each being healthy in mind and body (when not sun-struck), of sound family and good prospects, enlivened by wholesome ambition, of equal potential and service to our nation (albeit one a parliamentarian), then reason dictates that if one be sacrificed that the others might live, that would be of net gain—and far preferable to the demise of all three. And having proceeded that far, it is further obvious that the unselfish one would best be he of greatest size. For he could satisfy the others the most, yet would have made strong inroads to the collective larder if left alive as the largest mouth animated by the grossest appetite. As we sit disconsolately chewing the thongs with which we had been tied—it satisfies the habit of placing matter in the mouth, yields a salty meatiness and exercises the teeth—I announce to the others my regretable conclusion. I deploy the most indirect and diplomatic terms I can summon.

'It may interest you to know,' I say, 'whilst we are on the subject of food, to know that in Borneo the aboriginals eat human flesh. They name it long-pig. They value it highly. It is clear that there can be no more nutritious or complete diet for a person than a person. For the one contains exactly what the other needs, and in exactly the right proportions.'

Despite this devious circumlocution, they understand me well enough. We have slept together since the start of our expedition—having naturally reverted to our habits of school. Times and customs change, but in our day it was usual at Naval School to stow six scholars to a bed. There was a deficit of mattresses. It was held to foster proper naval sentiment. Yet this night, without discussion, we do not lie like porkers in a sty, but position ourselves some yards apart. I can see, piercing the gloom, the open pupils of my friends as we each think of Borneo. When we commence the next day's march, each keeps some distance from his fellows. We watch each other warily, reluctant to take a lead. Walking abreast, he in the centre feels unease—like piggy in the middle—and skirts his way to the side. It is saddening to see the spirit of the School diminished so.

Oistermaa, though never the most perspicacious of men, sees clearly the way in which the land lies. He tries to engage us in banter. Then, finding his feigned jollity ill-suited to the occasion, resorts to tones of self-pity, then braggartry. He speaks of being the only child of a frail-hearted mother, speculates gratuitously and immodestly on his political career, venturing that he might rise to Kabinet and find there a central chair. We listen to a tedious monologue in which he states a political philosophy. It is formed of the most bland and unexceptionable propositions, as though he were canvassing for our votes. He declaims on class, friends, King, nationhood and constitution. He has an economic theory in advance of being appointed Chancellor for Finance.

I stay silent and Bertii Smugsen says little, observing —pithily and sagaciously, I feel—that he is as good as the next man, only slightly less bulky than some.

We sit. Bertii and I have some unspoken rapport from which Oistermaa is excluded. He senses this for, after a painful pause in which he tries to catch our eyes, aiming smiles of sickly sycophancy, he stands, shakes us both by the hand, then stumbles on ahead.

We follow, watching the bobbling bald pate of his bowed head glisten crimson under the blazing sun—like the bull of an archery target.

Today I purchased this notebook to keep my journal and document my pharmacological researches and, after some preamble about my adventures in Aafryka, wrote 'Today I purchased this notebook to keep my journal and document my pharmacological researches and, after some preamble about my adventures in Aafryka wrote 'Today I purchased this notebook...' '

A man could fill the entire journal in this manner, which naturally prompts him to some speculations as to the algebra of recursiveness. This new problem aside, I feel quite jocular. If a mite languid. I shall go walk in King Ludwig Gardens and deploy my whistle. It emits shrill pulses, too arch for the human ear to hear. But passing dogs know me well enough, yelping and whining. Horses suddenly shy, depositing their riders. It is very droll. It amuses the children. Perhaps I should write to the War Ministry with details of this elegant and effective riposte to the cavalry charge.

How I am vexed. I cannot find the whistle. My wife has tidied it away, or else the parlour maid has stolen it. Neither come when I call. If I cannot take the whistle, it is not worth walking the park. I feel provoked and quite out of temper.

It occurs to me that I might find some concealment for the whistle (the world knows it as the Baa MindeBerg pitch-pipe) when I walk out with it. This would avoid the risk of suspicion or detection. It is often necessary for a scientist to conceal his practices for the sake of objectivity and precision. I have made a quick sketch how the pipe might be recessed within my cane and activated by air pressure from a bulb secreted in my arm pit. With this apparatus, I might continue my studies in the Royal Zoological Gardens. I have tested the hearing of the birds, reptilians and small mammals. Now remain the elephant, rhinoceros, hippopotamus and other gross mammals. I should not wish the attendants to know my purpose, lest I am ejected if the beasts rebel.

Florynse, the maid, will look oddly at me when she brings my afternoon tea. She will adamantly deny having taken my whistle. The tea will be but barely lukewarm which prompts me to speculate as to the effective design of a heat-retaining tea-pot. I think it facile enough to pack insulation around body and spout and seal it all up within an outer thermexclusive cover. Yet it has not occurred to the maid.

I should build such a pot and present it to my wife (it

might act the conversation piece when she entertains her friends) to accompany the agitation rods I designed to replace the spoons. Together they shall constitute the Baa MindeBerg Scientific Tea Apparatus.

Till I fixed upon the problem, all in the household had been happy enough with the tea spoon whose deficiencies passed unremarked or hidden. In truth it is a defective, wasteful instrument. Its distributive effects may be matched with considerably less effort by drawing a bevelled spatula twice through the beverage. When one considers the size of our nation, the sweetness of its tooth, the average tea consumption of each, the saving of productive energy would be immense. It is enough, I have calculated, to build a warship daily. It is a common feature of conventions and habits that they waste time and energy, applying the break to our national life. Gossip, the hand-shake, Feetball and Sauna all fit this principle—though they offer comforts enough to their adherents.

I have been considering Florynse's manner towards me. She blushes when she speaks, adverts her eyes, looks intently to her shins. She twists her hands together, writhing them in embarrassment. I fear the child has some infatuation. It is common enough for young women to favour a man of mature vigour.

She has willowy, wobbly legs, like a fawn newborn. Two freckles of dark amber lie snug below an ear. There's a tremble to her long pale neck. Her waist flares up to a heaving chest, down to the provocative arch of her hips. Standing against the light of the window, she shows off the shapes of her thighs through the translucence of her skirt. Through the glossy fissure of her moist lips breaks the tip of a coral tongue, frothed with saliva, quivering at the pursed, wet opening.

I told her firmly. She must ferry the tea more promptly from the kitchen.

I am not an unhandsome man. I am not, as some urchins shouted yesterday in the park, conspicuously short. As height is distributed amongst men, I may fall to the untall side of the median. But compared to some Pigmy tribes of Aafrykan forests—well documented in the *Geographical Gazette*—I am a veritable giant. There's thick, vigorous hair on both sides of my scalp. It's barely tinged by grey. If my ears promote themselves, bending outward to expose themselves to the frontal view, it is not to any extreme degree. It contributes to my air of eager intelligence.

People often comment on my eyes, which are strong and penetrative. They have a playful sparkle which aptly sketches my nature. I think it well known I'm an amiable man. I have heard none say otherwise—except my wife, who is prone to certain cyclical emotional disturbances which render her spiteful when she thinks herself slighted.

She has been prone to flamboyant melancholy. 'I now retire to my bed to die, Friedryk,' she announces grandly, 'You shall not see me alive again.' But I always do. For after a single day, or two at most, on her solitary deathbed, she feels much improved. Then all is well again for between ten and fourteen days.

Currently she shows distinct improvement. Her moodiness has been dispelled. And she has found a new friend—a Mr Aaskvist, nephew of the Governor of Upsyalii, an ineffectual young man, with whom she debates the merits of certain Florentine painters. She anticipates these aimless episodes with such pleasure that I cannot bring myself to dissuade her from the fatuous distraction.

9

Abstinence

2nd June

Marriage is much misunderstood. I never subscribed to that sentimental fallacy that asserts this contract a personal affair of two private parties. No. It has significance. It is a grand occasion—when Life plays hazard with sentient dice, at the crossroads of destinies.

It is the union of two families, each bearing the errands of nature and lessons of history. It requires of the couple that they act as agents for the powers of life which are invested in them. For we are the transients of history, brief butterflies of a summer's day whose mission is to the unborn. We are breeding stock. We must chose wisely, as wise life has chosen us.

So I did not seek passion in marriage. Nor did it leap out and surprise me there. I looked instead for a sound and fertile soil in which to plant my seed. There were several requirements I desired met by a spouse. She was to be of good pedigree, robust health, serene disposition, conventional good taste, clean and sturdy frame, sharp wit, but discreet and modest of word, untainted by gossip. Initial surveys disappointed. The excitement and pleasures of the chase would evaporate at the discovery of a dypsomaniacal brother, crippled cousin, a father who believes himself the reincarnation of Admiral Skyrnii, a sister who hallucinated or converted to Catholicism. There is much ill-health and eccentricity in our national stock. It seemed of prohibitive difficulty to find a clean, unsullied line of desent.

Then, alas, there were the girls themselves. I found women of good family and reputation only to discover in the subject in question a history of febrile convulsions, artistic nature, unwholesome passions, moral laxities, decayed teeth, forgetfulness, indifference, facetious or wilful temperament.

My researches were long and scrupulous. I thought I should never find a good woman. My habit of dropping a suitor when she and the family believed the courtship but barely begun gained me an undeserved reputation for fickle coldness. I was much misunderstood. Some thought me the Don Juan or dilettante. Supper tables began to close to me. Mothers spoke to me with icy reproof, fathers with tetchiness or irony.

I was forced to shift my scrutiny from our Capital to the provinces, but some reputation had ever preceded me.

I thought it sage to discover the background before approaching the girl. Here, my strategy again was amiss. On discovering no discrediting information, I would become excited and disclose too early my purpose.

'Do you think we should be well-matched as man and wife?' I would ask, eager to learn of the girl's true feelings.

Sometimes the reply was scathing. I suffered some wounding words. I particularly remember the gratuitous rudeness of Hanna Moikliimaastiirpi, daughter of the Bishop of Peligfors.

'We have not been introduced, 'she said, 'and I have no plans for marriage. But should I ever need a man—to carry my cases or shoe my horse—I should not choose a bald, red, dwarf. In truth, I find them so unsightly.'

It was with some spiteful pleasure that I later learned she had married a composer of comic operas and led a poor parochial life in Papskii Prospect.

Alyse was not striking but defined by a wholesome normality. This was to the good. Beautiful women attract attention and can cause difficulties between men. She was not pretty nor ugly, not stout nor thin, neither clever nor stupid, not dark nor light. Her face and figure were well constructed on average proportions, neither flattered by a dazzle of beauty nor tainted by uncomeliness. There was nothing unusual in her features, nothing striking in her manner or demeanour. She regarded me with a proper politeness, without either encouraging or disdaining my attentions. She answered discreetly my questions about herself and family without resorting to any excesses of candour or concealment. Her interests were held without vehement force. She wisely stopped short of enthusiasms. These sometimes disfigure a woman. Those rare opinions she voiced were sound and carefully phrased, uninflated by eloquence and entirely uncluttered by wit. I felt confident I could mould her well.

She played the piano with moderate enthusiam, not well but not badly. At bridge she showed judgement and memory of quite adequate order but was innocent of guile. She would no more finesse than a walrus might waltz. On the tennis court her coordination and stamina were of average soundness. She did not dispute my calls—even when I tried to provoke her with absurd rulings or peremptorily changed the laws of the game. She found no unhealthy pleasure in winning points. When she found me out of position, she gently lobbed back the ball to my forehand slash.

There was nothing unnatural about either her passions or posture.

She seemed perfectly marriageable. Nothing I learned subsequently in our courtship diminished the high esteem in which I held her.

'When we are married, Alyse, I should need to feel free to travel.'

'Marry, Friedryk?'

'To Aafryka,' I said, 'and to points East. I should wish that you had no objections to this, nor to my keeping animals.'

'The East, Friedryk?'

'Marsupials, I explained, 'woolly monkeys. Small mammalians and some amphibians. They would be kept at a sanitary distance from our living quarters.'

'Living quarters?'

'There will be a town house in Helikfors, a summer house by the lakes and, of course, the family estate. I should wish to entertain friends and scholarly colleagues. We should consume wine and spirits in moderation. You should have maid, cook and gardener. A butler is unnecessary.' She listened with quiet attention. It is dishonest of her to now dispute our avowed agreements.

'There will be no carpets.'

'No carpets?'

'Carpets are a fallacy,' I explained this clearly at the time, 'they collect dust and dirt which irritate my respiratory tracts.'

She had, and still retains, this enigmatic gesture of smiling without humour and hoisting her eyebrows. It was an oversight. I did not then take the precaution of ascertaining the meanings of this gesture. I know now.

'We should like several children, though my masculine needs are moderate.' She blushed, though not excessively. We did understand each other.

'The Baa MindeBergs hunt—badger, fox, snipe and cormorant. But this is not required of the women.'

And so, our bargaining completed, promises made— having reached an amiable accord that we should live in harmony with respect for each other—I approached the father to disclose my intentions. He asked of me certain questions, concerning my background and health, that in other circumstances might have seemed impertinent. He was unfamilar with the reputation of the Baa MindeBergs for robust productivity. He seemed much concerned with certain aspects of my mind that had been reported to him.

In my final year at the Grosse Collegium, while preparing for the Mathematical papers, I strained my brain through excessive and unremitting indulgence in algebra. Anyone of a mechanical bent cannot help but recognise the manifold similarities between brain and engine. Both may

13

last a lifetime of sensible use, empower and pull great loads. Yet both suffer malfunction, straining and grinding their gears when excessive burdens are placed upon them. My engine was widely respected at the Collegium for its formidable speed and power. However, the strains and loads I forced it to carry caused it some temporary damage. Hair-spring mechanisms became dislocated from their precise bearings, impeding the thrusts of the pistons. The chambers became clogged with unburned residues which smouldered, causing foul emissions. The fumes became choking and I was unable to carry any but the lightest mental loads. I was forced to garage my engine and enlist the attentions of a competent mechanic. This compelled me to abandon my Mathematical studies. Instead, I quickly prepared for the papers in Natural Sciences. These subjects making relatively slight demands on the mind, and re-quiring only memory and method, I was still able to obtain my Certificate of Excellence, First Class.

Some six years later, when I thought it fully repaired, my brain again suffered malfunction. By some misfortune of timing, this coincided with the illness, then death, of my mother of whom I was peculiarly fond. My vision was affected and I saw sights that are not available in the material world. Unknown voices spoke to me in abusive or hectoring terms, instructing me against my will. I suffered some confusions as to my true identity. Perhaps I had con-tracted some malaise on my foreign travels which was slow to manifest its debilitating powers. Else I was unused to transporting those cargoes of emotion loaded upon me by the demise of my parent. I am happier and more competent, with problems of logic and number than with those of passion and feeling. Accordingly, I try to restrict my trading on the markets of emotion. Each must find his specialism and apply there his best energies.

I explained all this to Alyse's father who seemed favourably well impressed by my accounts of my stability. Yet in so doing, I must have raised doubts as to the depth of my feelings.

'Do you love my daughter?' he asked, quite bluntly. He used those very words; which I thought intrusive.

Well, I had spent but little time in her company, having barely handled any parts of her but both knees and her right hand. My arm had accidentally brushed her right breast, confirming it was firm and sound. Having consulted her family physician, I had not thought it credulous to take the rest of her on trust, from external cues to inner depths— the bulges and curves of clothing, and so on. I felt her still a stranger. But I knew nothing to her disfavour. She was the only marriageable woman I had met. I knew of no higher compliment, so conceded to the father that I did indeed love her. I further added that in my explorations in Aafryka and the East I had gained some rich experiences. Some of these involved women. So that having sown some oats, I was now ready to cultivate the golden grains of domesticity. I wished to breed, I explained, and paid him some pretty compliments on the excellence of his stock. I sensed this flattered him and that it was required of me to speak more and warmly of his daughter. I referred enthusiastically to her lack of any physical disability, her mental soundness, the ivory of her teeth, straightness of her limbs, clearness of her gaze, the sheen of her hair, the perfect adequacy of her intellect, the respectability of her kin.

This done, we had tea and talked of Egypt. The ladies joined us. Alyse played some melody on the piano without any evident mistakes. Each for their own reasons was happy enough. It was thus I won my wife.

Yet how I wander from the matter in hand. I have wasted an hour in aimless jottings. Tomorrow, I shall continue in earnest my investigation of pharmaceuticals.

I am a methodical man. I have my system. Through the pages of Moeller's *Pharmacopeia* I have marked out all those chemicals which promise some mental interest—lubrication, speeding, slowing, sensitising or blunting of the engine of a man's mind. I shall proceed alphabetically, and dose myself with each drug on the route, and properly note all effects in this book. I believe myself the first man to attempt this.

But first I must feed the monkey. Then I shall walk the park. After, I shall compute some mathematics of recursiveness to work up an appetite for supper.

Perhaps, tonight, Alyse will wish to enjoy my body: for she has not had me recently.

Abtzmyer's Mushroom

4th June

This pretty fungus, broad on a squat stalk, with a purple skin ornamented by yellow blotches, has been commended to me in the unsolicited correspondence of a Herr Mueller of Leipzig—who writes, in deranged German, lacking in syntax but rich in adjectival colour, that this mushroom, dried, shredded and eaten, takes a man's perception on exotic vacation.

I have now been able to acquire a small sample, some few grammes, from the Curator at Queen Maathilde Gardens. In return, I offered him some small change and timely advice on the care of his monoecius Gymnospermae.

It is quite chewy, a curious admixture of the putrid and the nutty. There is an aftertaste of claret and bouquet of violets. In all, it is compelling.

Alyse bemuses me. I can find no satisfactory explanation. It is most perplexing, and quite unorthodox, for a decent woman, long and contentedly married to a distinguished Royal Academician, to be found (by this husband) in the act of clutching a hand (the right) of an effete, idle, unprepossessing young man whose sole distinction is a distant kinship to the Governor of Upsalyii. They were huddled tight on the marital sofa, engrossed in steady mutual gaze, speaking, the one to the other, yet so quietly—as if exchanging confidences—that I could not catch their words. Their lips were so close as to almost touch.

I pretended that there was nothing untoward and spoke

nonchalantly of the habits of Benajymyn, monkey. The circulation of blood to their faces rose rapidly, then slowly subsided. Mr Aaskvist voiced a stammer I had never heard before. Alyse enquired with warmth and concern of the state of my amphibians. She is usually less interested.

When they thought my gaze distracted, they looked again to each other. Mr Aaskvist elevated his eyebrows in a silly and effeminate gesture. Alyse gulped and blinked simultaneously in the manner of a common frog (*Rana Temporaria*).

I made myself busy, aligned and interrogated a range of plausible hypotheses. Yet none fits the facts of the case, nor explains the curious phenomenon of manual intimacy.

I went so far as to suspect that there might exist between them some bond of affection in excess of the calls of platonism and shared concern for the artefacts of the Italian Renaissance. But this will not do. She's a married woman. Her husband a vigorous, kindly man and distinguished scholar. Their marriage rests on the firmest foundations of warmth and respect. They have the welfare of their joint progeny foremost to their hearts. Besides, the second party to the hand-shake was but a boy of limp, languid and effete appearance. Why with his long yellow wavy hair, swollen ruby lips and slender frame, he might even pass for a girl.

It is a perplex, teasing my taste for conundrum. There will be some simple solution. Yet, so far, it evades me.

This mushroom, too, poses many questions. Upon a second dose, its flavours are quite transformed. It becomes crunchy and gives up the flavours of roast ox and pomegranate. There is, nonetheless, clearly something to it of the qualities of smoked haddock and strawberries. When I chew upon its changing textures, it scuds and squits about my mouth, prickling here and tickling there. It resounds in the mouth. Its sounds are those of a bow being drawn harshly across the strings of a cello, or else, of the squeezing of an asthmatic accordion. In either case, there is no difficulty in playing the opening bars of Haydn's oboe concerto. The secret lies in exact control of the tempi. All chewing must be purple and squelchy.

I had failed to notice the pungent odours of my chamber. The desk wafts a breeze of nutmeg. My boots smell of calves' liver, braised with onions. Sage and tarragon leak from the lamp. From this pen comes a shaft of mint, wrestling to overpower the stench of rotting apples from my notebook. The clock strikes crushed raspberries. It is three of the afternoon, and very fruity. But my nostrils advise that some crustaceans had stowed away beneath my desk, reeking a stench of fishy death.

'Your tea, Sir,' says Florynse, in her crisp aquamarine voice. I can smell the gravy of her breath. Yet from the rest of her comes a stronger taint.

'Why, child, have you been bathing in anchovy sauce?' 'Sir?' She blushes a vulgar puce. The pores of her forehead yawn open to weep aniseed. She is quite obtuse and almost rhomboid. I count her axes of parallax. Yet the angles of convergence shift. Her knees crackle with static.

'You are oscillating, Florynse, around a shifting centre of gravity. Pray, stop it. It offends the laws of geometry and it certainly irritates me.'

But she continues to frisk and shake. Yellow flashes shoot lurid from her hips.

'Why do your nipples stare at me so?' I ask, for she has fixed me with harsh, unblinking breasts, ogling through her starched apron. 'Has no one advised you it is rude?'

I invite her to sit on my lap and sniff my waistcoat—for it carries the fragances of beeswax and lavender. But she just stands there, her chest throbbing, her lips inflating, and starbursts breaking golden from the filaments of her hair. Her thighs crackle. She dances brazenly, quite naked beneath her clothing.

'You are yellow and argent, today, Florynse.' I like to give credit where it is due. 'Rest the gravity of your condition upon my lap. Come sit on me. I yearn to listen to your eyes. I wish to sniff at your innocence then touch your credulity.'

But the child was gone. And I laid down my pen.

There is much to report and more to conclude. For this is a busy, engrossing little mushroom.

I regret that whilst intoxicated, and absentee landlord of my person, I may have made some remarks to a domestic servant which might be misconstrued as bearing unseemly overtones, pink and purple, rather greasy. I shall remind the girl of the terms of her employment, and require her confidentiality.

The fungus must have powerful aphrodisiacal properties to have moved me so from protocol. For I am not a licentious man. I am not prone to molesting servants; but have been embarrassed by a persuasive mushroom.

There are men of my class—gentlemen of the foremost families even—who visit bordellos to converse with prostitutes, commission the procurement of virgins, engage in unnatural acts, search out what is most lewd, sully the procreative act. I have never been thus.

My visits to brothels have been but occasional, in service of research, or else simply for the brief relief of a physiological compulsion when my wife has been so far disabled by melancholy, indifference or illness to satisfy my reasonable requirements. I have, in the main, patronised that respectable parlour of Mrs Vysinmaa's which serves the hygienic appetites of the clergy and civil service. I favour there Siigi, Inge or Britte, and will touch none other—save Agnas or Emmi. All are decent girls practised in meeting my modest requirements. They refrain from vulgar language and are clean in their habits and person. If a man discounted their trade, he would find all of them quite decent.

I am not a man to chase or molest a maid. I have been misled by a fungus.

Awaking at six-thirty from a deep reverie, I found myself quite naked with incomplete remembrance of the intervening hours. This fungus disturbs the senses. It induces hallucinations—of taste and smell—evokes visions, including flashing lights of gold and yellow. The senses become twisted and confused. Sights have sounds, sound has colour, colour has texture, and texture provokes sights which yield smells.

To cite one example: my voice is yellow and sounds trumpets, which smell cheesey. It is a velvety cheese of brownish hardness, grunting...

All is quite diverting, being married to all else, or mother to the other. I retain a memory of touching my body on various parts to produce sounds, playing—with scratching, rubbing, stroking and tweaking—certain excerpts from Monsieur Bizet's Carmen, including the Gypsy and Toreador songs from Act 2 and the final chorus of Act 4. It struck me as a perplexing choice. This vulgar opera has never been a favourite of mine.

I fear I hallucinated Florynse, naked and voluptuous, playing our national anthem upon her belly with my tongue. This was accompanied by the welling of certain erotic sensations I had not known were in me.

The room took to an independent will thereafter. There was a deal of shaking, hurling and swirling around me. I fell, as if from the highest cliff, to the embrace of rocks below. Awaking from this death, I found swarms of red and green ants treating me as highway, pausing to picnic on my flesh. Their pincers were needles. All of this was painful. As was the gnawing of rats at my legs.

At some later stage—it seemed that painful years had intervened—my consciousness returned to an awareness of this room. I was here addressed by a disembodied voice. He made accusations and insinuations, having some intimate information of me, which he twisted to weave ingenious slanders. I was forced to vigorous disputation to defend my good name.

'Murderer, cannibal,' he hissed. He had the accent of a gentleman which made his insults seem all the stranger.

Now, I am prepared to debate with any man, provided he be well informed of the issues and is adequately armed with evidence. I am prepared to consider all manner of natural or abnormal phenomena, even to entertain apparitions. So it was not his nonexistence which angered me but his familiarity of whispering behind my left ear. That and the frank, unsubstantiated rudeness of his remarks.

I remained silent, pretending he was not there—which, in truth, was the case. This irritated him. He retaliated by whistling, chuckling and cackling. He seemed to know just how best to annoy me.

'Some say you are Royal Academician.' This he said in a most reasonable and cultured tone.

'It is true. And I am Chairman of the Institute of Geography.'

'But you are rogue and plagiarist.'

'I am not.' Too late, I realised, he had lulled me into conversation with his brief display of civility.

'You are excrement. You are a thought-thief. You purloined the work of Hoosins.'

'There are facial similarities between our papers on small mammals,' I explained, 'but the chronology is clear. I published first.' He would not catch me with that stale charge. I had answered it often enough before.

'You haunt brothels,' he clucked.

'I do not.' I visit one such house, and that for my research.

'You are a lewd, bald, one-legged dwarf.'

'I have more substantial form than you,' I laughed, for I am sharp in argument, 'and have more hair. And two more legs.' For I was not going to suffer the irony of having some phantom sneer at my physique.

He persisted in this manner, assembling a range of slanders concerning my integrity, temperament and manliness. I chose to ignore him and was delighted to discover that with time, as the effects of the mushroom diminished, he grew less loud, and was forced to shouting to have himself heard at all. He continued ranting in the distance till I had quite left him behind me. I can say, without immodesty, I got the better of the argument.

Then, retrieving my trousers from the gas lamp, my

shirt from the bookshelf, and my smoking jacket from the shoulders of the gibbon skeleton, I dressed and made myself smart.

I have detected a problem attendant upon pharmacological research. I was unimaginative not to anticipate it. It is of disentangling those events that precede intoxication from those that follow from it. Surely, I must resolve this, if I am to drug myself daily.

I have some memory—and, indeed, some note in this journal—of finding Alyse in manual intimacy with Mr Aaskvist. Yet I am now unclear if this was hallucination or actuality. The sheer improbability of the occurrence leads me to suppose the former. Further, I have asked Alyse and she quite denies any such event. She was much outraged and aggrieved. It took a deal of time and patience to appease her. Perhaps I might contrive a new appliance to soothe her.

It is of advantage to my wife that she is married to a distinguished and enterprising scientist of the first rank. For I have provided her with a variety of domestic novelties, making a range of hygienic, functional and efficient interventions in the management of our household.

Ours, I flatter myself, is the the only home in our nation with an electric water-closet. A red sign, illuminated outside, and duplicated in the living room, signals occupancy of the chamber. This spares embarrassment. The water flushes warm. This prevents the system from freezing in winter. A simple system of gears, clutch and brake, harnessed to a six horse-power engine, raises and lowers the seat to suit the comfort and shape of the user. Contrary to Alyse's complaints, the apparatus is easy to drive, after but little practice, and the engine no noisier than others of its type. The pressing of a lever causes sanitary papers to waft down from a vent in the ceiling on to the lap of the occupant.

23

Our letter-box was so designed that the insertion of any package caused a sign to be raised—thanking the post-man and wishing him good day. But my orifice was so admired, I was forced to seal it up. For the neighbours' children would push all manner of insanitary and unwanted items through the hole, just to enjoy the rise of my sign.

To avoid the risk of respiratory infections, caused by the build up of dust and dirt, I have eliminated all carpets, curtains and tapestries. Curtains are the bane of our culture causing untold bronchial suffering.

When Alyse made some casual complaint about the hardness of her pillows, I replaced them that day with inflatable water cushions. It was a considerable relief to be freed from duck-down which acts promiscuous host to small particles of detritus.

To my wife's bed I have fitted a series of cogs and cranks. Merely by turning the lever through a few rotations, it is possible to raise the head or foot of the bed, or to contrive a cosy and comforting valley in the centre.

When she finds that I have ventured to her bed chamber and set the mattress true to the horizontal, Alyse knows that I intend to visit her that night. If I hear her—my ears pressed to the dividing wall—rotating the cranks to some other position, I know that she would prefer that I shouldn't. Alas, Alyse is more fond of the levers of late.

So is the physiology of our marriage signalled by the semaphore of cog wheels. It is irregular. But it spares useless and hurtful debate.

It might be supposed that I—having enjoyed the carnal act in four continents, with the women of twenty-six tribes or nations, of a variety of shapes, ages, colours and customs, in a great range of postures, in the glare of sun and glimmer of moon, in beds, canoes, wattle huts, lagoons, millet fields, under tables, in cupboards, and (once) upon the back of an elephant (*Loxodonta Aafrykana*) and so knowing all that is possible in coupling, what expected of man and required of woman, what pleasurable

and what unsatisfying, what universal and what parochial—might have particularly valuable and informative
instruction to deploy in the conjugal bed by virtue of such
thorough researches. It might be supposed that an
inexperienced young wife might defer to her husband's
expertise in these matters, see what had to be learned and
eagerly study his lessons. But no. It was not so. Within
brief months of our marriage, she commenced to contest
my instruction, veto this, scoff at that, order me in the
deployment of my limbs, insinuate portions of her person
to my attention, push me here and prod me there. In short,
she man-handled me. And she would talk—not brief
endearments, or terse yelps of pleasure, but extended
monologues, sometimes of the matters to hand, but also of
entirely coincidental concerns.

'The maid, Friedryk, is very droll... Your hand,
Friedryk, not so, but thus...And the window, Friedii? Did
you close it?. No, Friedii. More gently...Just so, Diikii. Yes
there...*Allegro* Ikii, *ma non troppo.*'

I found it facetious and unsettling. I told her so. Did she
change her ways? She did not. She said I was fusty.

To make quite sure, I consulted three dictionaries and
then re-examined my own conduct. There could be no
mistake. I was not fusty. I am not fusty. Alyse is so
infuriatingly inexact in her terminology. It can quite
undermine the sensible intercourse of man and wife.

For the sake of variety, to shift her from habitual
patterns, and because it's an unlikely and educative
practice, I thought to teach her the Amanque convention of
the Azonquitte Indians.

'In Papya, when man and wife are married,' I explained,
rotating her body to the correct posture.

'But Friedryk!' she squirmed back to her former position,
casting aside the feather, chicken head and plantains I had
carefully arranged to their exact places, and wearing an
infuriating smile of smug defiance, 'we are not Hotten-
tots.'

Some solecisms are too gross to pass unremarked. I was forced to explain the difference between Azonquitte and Hottentot. They inhabit different continents. But having said as much, and a little more, the procreative urge had quite left me.

'In Helikfors, the younger daughters of retired grain-merchants do it thus,' and she hugged my face into her thick cotton night gown.

The fault was partly mine, for I did exert a proper husbandly hand to quell her rebellion. And so, slowly and inexorably, we built between us a great wall of awkward-ness from small bricks of embarrassment.

Yet, to be married, man and wife must assert their bond. So it is that I venture, of an evening, to my wife's room and adjust the cranks to her bed. And she, I hear through the wall in my adjacent chamber, shifts them back or leaves them so.

We have had our outcomes. Alyse has been delivered of four children. The first, a boy, perished in his first week from respiratory frustration. The chest has ever been the Achilles Heel of the Baa MindeBergs. He was born scarlet but soon turned blue: his tiny chest heaving to grasp some leverage on air. We buried him Hiirbert.

But there is Friedryk, Siigrid and Bertii. I speak to them of an evening and instruct them at their lessons. The child is an impressionable creature. Early attention pays dividends. Friedryk is a decent enough chappie. There is nothing fundamentally wrong with him save his leaden dullness of mind. It is on Bertii I build my hopes. Though not yet six, he know the Greek and much enjoys Herodotus. In his aptitude for Mathematics he has learned some proofs of Euclid's. I am teaching him the proper classification of animals. He may grow to share my talents for science.

Siigrid resembles her mother, so I am quite devoted to her.

Alcohol

5th June

I am no stranger to drink. As other men of my station, who can so afford to keep moistened their proclivities, I enjoy a brace of bottles, of Bordeaux or Burgundy, with dinner, and after may relax with a decanter of brandy. On occasions, I have consumed to such excess that the words have not pranced through my mind or tripped from my tongue as nimbly and eagerly as they ought.

I first gained the thirst and the taste and the practice at school, for ale was served with the evening meal, and for lunch on Saturdays. Wines and spirits had to be purchased by the crate from the mess. But these were of inferior quality and discredit to the school. So I instructed my wine merchant to deliver as my needs arose.

Often, when I had washed his shirt and ironed his trousers, polished his boots, filled the scuttle with firewood, and burnished his athletics trophies, Oistermaa (may he rest in peace) would invite me to come lie on the floor of his study.

We spear muffins on the poker and toast them at the fire. The coals flare and the buns char. The heat is so fierce, here by the grate, that we are compelled to strip ourselves of clothes and laze naked on the rug. Oistermaa opens a bottle of brandy. We scoff the best part, swilling from the bottle, letting the juice spill on our skin. We are ferocious in our appetities as boys often are. The drink affects him the more, strongly, if not profoundly, and he grows quite maudlin, stroking my thighs, nuzzling my shoulders, rubbing his chest next to mine, slurring pleasantries in my ear. His hands and mind wander crazily, as the drink works its way. He becames so sodden as to suffer the delusion that I am woman. He seems now in his cups, oblivious to the patent difference between boy and girl, and tries to improvise upon me as best he can. So we are moved to wrestle— he to pursue the delusion, I to disabuse him. He is the stronger, but I the more sober. This leads to an even contest. We much enjoy the athletics and exercise, for we are both keen sports. Eager. Strong. Fierce.

I remember thinking then of the curious and manifold effects of alcohol—that it rendered men sentimental, blurred their vision, slurred their speech, blunted their movements, provoked them to unfortunate liaisons, and sometimes, disabled them from completing their impluse. I learned also that I was relatively resistant to the effects, being possessed of an enviable capacity. For when Oistermaa lay snorting and spent, I would cover him with a rug, finish the bottle, then go compute some algebra with a fresh and lucid mind.

But we have grown indifferent, Bacchus and I, from long familiarity, like man and wife who find no excitements or mysteries remain, but rest together by habit, held in the clutch of convention. I have read of this in novels and seen it enacted upon the popular stage.

It is not that she no longer moves me. She does. But she no longer transports me. I yearn to feel anew the touch she once had. Before she felt feeble from familiarity.

Yet any stale partnership may be revived. I intend to penetrate beyond sobriety, to rediscover those landscapes of drunkenness that so entertained my youth. It is but a matter of upping the intake to cajole a jaded taste. I consulted Hoosins on this.

'How may a man get truly drunk?' I asked, 'Properly pickled, thick as a tick, fur-brained, foozlified, conflummoxed and cherubimical?'

'The best part of a bottle of brandy should do it. You

must take it internally.' He said, 'I've gone that far down the tipium grove, beyond is off my chart."

I explained that I had ventured further, yet without the same rewards. Hoosins was sympathetic, advising that I should try intermixing my drinks—saying that a rotation between vodka, brandy and schnapps might work the trick. Alcohol, he advised, is more readily absorbed on an empty stomach. So for the sake of my science, I forsook smoked pork and duck eggs for breakfast, braised veal and poached trout for luncheon. Hoosins also reported, what I had never known before, the quickest way to insobriety is in the sauna. One needs only to pour a bottle of vodka over the hot stones. The alcohol is absorbed through the skin—saving a man from the labour of repeatedly raising a glass. It is a different sensation, he informs me, when the entirety of the body is squiffled. Why, even his pizzle is pissed. But if a man does not want to remove all his clothes, then he might beat his back with birch twigs, and immerse his feet in cold water - so speeding the distribution of alcohol in the body by provoking the circulation. Serious drinkers and alcoholics insist on a cold bath between bottles, Hoosins advised me. This is why, he reports, they are often to be seen rolling in snow when no bathroom is available.

'What interesting psychic effects might arise, if I succeeded so far as to get squarely squiffled?'

He listed feelings of euphoria, a deadening of pain, lessening of worry, increased capacity of song, unnecessary affection for others. He assured me that the effects can be intensified if only one stands on one's head. I took this last suggestion as a sample of that facetiousness to which he is so particularly prone.

Hoosins was so unusually cheerful and warm, I suspected he had been drinking himself.

'Don't forget,' he waved down from the steps of Bryke's Club, 'iced water, birch twigs and headstands.' Then he announced loudly to all passers-by, breaching a confidence, quite unnecessarily I thought, 'Count Friedryk Baa

MindeBerg, Royal Academician, is now going home to get rolling drunk.'

There gaze back at me three distorted reflections of my face, leering, stretched grotesquely around the curved bottles. It is disquieting, reminding me that there is something to my appearance that attracts the curiosity or derision of others.

In King Ludwig Gardens people stare at me strangely if I greet them. They smile politely enough, but when they are passed they whisper and look backward at me. I know this because I watch them carefully, to properly record their reactions. Nor is it just people. Herring gulls single me out for special contempt. They slow their wings, gliding slow above, in order to deposit their excreta upon my hat and shoulders. I have computed the probabilities.

let x = area of Ludwig Gardens; let y = area of F.B.M.'s hat and shoulders; let n = number of gulls in gardens; let s = frequency of excretory impulse of average gull.

let Baa MindeBerg and gulls be randomly distributed within the boundaries of the Garden—

Clearly, $(y/x) \times (n/s)$ cannot conceivably exceed three times this week. For it is a large place and these birds cannot crap the whole day long.

It is obvious that I am hit more frequently than mere chance should allow. And yesterday a Snipehund crossed Syrkii Prospect just to bark at me. Indeed, he crossed the wide street for this purpose alone; to follow me yapping and snapping. It was quite perturbing for this is normally the most amiable and sanguine breed of dog. I cannot discern what it is to my appearance that wins me such derisive reviews. The dog's master came trotting after us to reclaim his cur, which then wagged its tail wildly, frothed saliva upon his boots, then shook itself. The man scowled at me, as though I were the culprit beast.

'Good boy, Albii.' he said, bald and brazen as that. And turned on his heels before I thought to protest. I do not know what all this means—unless both of them were rabid.

Benjamyn, my woolly monkey, was cool and disinterested—verging upon insolence—when I visited him this morning. He quite turned his back on me, pretending a preoccupation with his xylophone. Alyse and Florynse are also offhand.

It is not the case that I have only one leg. People are so rudely inexact. If I had but one leg, I should admit so. There would be no shame in it. Often a man may lose a part of himself through no fault of his own. As it happens, I have one and three-quarter legs: as close to two as makes no difference. The left was severed just above the ankle, and the lesser part mislaid in Aafryka.

I devoted much time and effort to the design of a surrogate foot. It functions excellently. Apart from my slight limp, there is nothing to alert the world that I have less than the full complement and length of limbs.

I think it unkind of children to follow me shrieking and giggling. I have told them so, but they do not desist. They hop behind, acting gross parodies of amputees—a chain of seven or eight of them, in single file, snaking behind me. The bolder ones amongst them invite me to join them in a game of Feetball. I know they ask only because I am technically ineligible, and because they are ironists.

I decline. For I have played with them the once before. That was sufficient. Though I had started well enough. Dribbling towards the goal, I rounded one defendist, and elbowed away another. Ambition flirted with confidence and I endeavoured to strike a score from some distance. The ball flew straight and hard enough—but my foot followed it, arching a slower parabolic curve to the hedge, in which he lodged. Having lost a foot, I was disabled in my attempts to recover it. The children were less than fully helpful. I have noted a similar compound difficulty with my spectacles. Having mislaid them, it is hard to see to recover them.

31

I doubt it contributes to the dignity and reputation of the Royal Academy if one of its most distinguished members acts the fool for children in King Ludwig Gardens. So I explained that I did not wish to play Feetball. Instead, I showed them my whistle, blew it to prove it was silent, then spoke a brief and elementary lecture on the science of acoustics. Then I gave them nine ffenyngs that they might go purchase the *Geographical Record* and read of the recent explorations of Patagonia.

Despite having consumed the best part of two bottles of spirits, dunking my foot in chill water, beating my abdomen with twigs, I have as yet no glimpses of any novel vistas of drunkenness. Rather, I feel quite nauseous. My mind is clear, but my body is reluctant to obey instructions. My legs buckle at the knees when I require them to transport me. 'Walk,' I bid them. It is little enough to ask of them. I pay them for no less.

Having vomited twice, I feel sufficiently improved to drink more and venture further. But I am a dirty, loathsome man. I have retched on the *Dieffenbachia Picta Exotica*.

I am a lucky man. Alyse is a good wife. Hoosins is a good friend. Cook is a good cook. My children are decent enough. They are too young for sensible conversation; but it is not their fault, but a consequence of their age and a stage they must pass through. I am a lucky man. I have more than I deserve. I am Royal Academician. I have several deserved reputations. The Queen appointed me adviser to the Royal Menagerie and awarded me Membership of the Order Ludwig. She gave me a sash. She is a kind Queen and more that I deserve. Queeny is my darling.

Alas, I have retched again. It is a decent enough *Dieffenbachia* and means no harm. It deserves better from a biologist. I am a loathsome man and I am prompted to speculate. I am a squat, bald man with but one foot to stand on. Alyse is a fine-looking woman. She has several attractive features about her and both her feet on the

32

ground. Between us, we have three feet. This is marriage. Man and woman share all that they have. On those nights I find myself in Alyse's bed, a sneak a glimpse beneath the covers. I can see four legs, three feet and a stump. I pretend that two of the feet are mine. For I borrow Alyse's left foot. In the morning I return it to her promptly. She does not even know I've used it. She is a good wife and I do not deserve her.

If I had my life again, I would do all that I have done. Everything. But I would not eat Oistermaa—who was a good friend but a poor larder. I would be kinder to Alyse who is a good wife.

Yet she is wrong to say my foot smells. She was talking of the right one—the fleshy foot, not the wooden one with brass fittings and padded leather toes. I have sniffed my proper foot. It has a slight aroma such is natural and fitting for a foot. To condemn it as smelly is to waltz with hyperbole. Is it likely that the author of *The Natural History of Marsupials*, and *Science of Human Faculties* would have an insanitary foot? A man welcome to the highest houses of society? Surely, another would have spoken to him of his foot before.

So it is unkind and insensitive of Alyse to cast suspicions on my one good foot. She is ever finding fault. I doubt she understands me. Else she would not say what she does.

I should be the master in my own house. If I wish to research pharmaceuticals, she should not complain. It is science, which is my profession, and the peak of man's achievement. It is little to ask that she fetches iced water and beats me with twigs. If she will not, she should not prevent the maid from helping in her stead.

So I have a hostile wife and uncooperative maid. Very well, I shall beat myself. I can do it the better.

Did Archimedes have to ask his wife before he took a bath? Was Mrs Diogenes ever fussing in her husband's barrel? Did Newton plead leave to visit the orchard?

They have hidden my bottles. I have but half a decanter of brandy remaining. They have taken all else. It is fortunate I am a versatile man. Were I not ingenious, I could venture no further upon this trail of drink.

They are not men of science—Alyse and Florynse. Their pharmacology is risibly slight. They think to stop me drinking by hiding my bottles and locking my door. Why, they might as well have posted a dypsomaniac to a distillery.

For an alcoholical, this study of mine would be an enchanted land. All around me, shelf upon shelf, lie my samples—glass jars radiant as a rainbow. There are tree frog, dogfish, marsupial parts, monkey brains, turtle eggs, Siamese twins in eternal embrace, the snout of a Hudson's Hydrax. All awash in their own solution, into which they bleed their subtle hues and leak their ripe flavours. There is enough pure alcohol here, Alyse, for two battalions of Swedish Guards to celebrate the Oswald Settlement and thereafer pickle their horses.

The Manchurians value it to combat rheumatism. I should never select it in preference to brandy. But, with quinine water for flavouring, tincture of grass-snake is not unpleasant. It may be true it is an acquired taste, yet I have the leisure to gain it.

But it is quite improper for maid and mistress to campaign against their master and steal his bottles. They have done it before. They shall not make it a habit. Later, I shall remonstrate. But now I feel fit for a sleep.

Ale

6th June

My forays of yesterday have left me numbed and weak. I'm resolved to drink no alcohol but small beer. As I had supposed, after but a few bottles I feel much improved.

Browsing the shelves in Foyiil's Scientific Book Emporium, I chanced upon Hoosins' slim new volume. I had not expected him to dedicate it to me, his friend—he chose instead his daughter. But I was perplexed to find in the index that I merited a mere five entries. Two of these were tinged with criticism. The book seemed to offer no serious advance so that, instead of purchasing it, I felt confident I might skim it briskly, there and then, in the thirty-four minutes I had available to me, and probably be none the wiser. But I was interruped in this by a smiling face, familiar, long-nosed—in profile reminiscent of an Echidna (*Tachyglossus Aculeatus*).

'This is a coincidence, Baa. I have just seen your very pretty wife,' he said, by which time I had quite remembered his name. It was Duckstaadt, Professor of Geography at the National Collegium. Occasionally, he had dined with us. 'She was walking the Heritage Museum with Mr Aaskvist and his sister Inge.'

'I fear you are mistaken,' I said briskly, hoping he might go away. I detest disturbance in a library.

'But no, Baa. It was she.'

I suspected him of purpose. He radiated a quite gratuitous amusement and gazed expectantly at me. I think he wished to tell me something he would not speak. He beamed down and studied my face, as though examining the creases of my forehead for his National Survey.

'My wife has many attractive features. She is very personable. She is a good mother to our children. In her best health, freed from any lingering melancholy, she inhabits a region close to prettiness. Yet it would be quite inexact to call her very pretty. That would suggest a cruel use of irony.'

'Nonetheless, it was Alyse—in a most vivacious mood, smiling and laughing.' So I took his observation as yet another instance of how a man tars another with his own brush, seeing his own characteristics in all others.

I laid down my book to explain: 'Then it certainly was not her.' I said, 'My wife seldom smiles. She never laughs. I know. I am her husband.'

I bade him good-day and returned to Hoosin's monograph. In his prose style, he borrows from the structures of porridge. I should have thought no more of my wife. But on my return, I met her in the hall. She addressed me there, telling me that she had visited the Gallery.

'Did it make you laugh?' I asked, feigning a slight disinterested enquiry.

'Certainly not, Friedryk. It is a Cathedral to Art.'

So it is all quite perplexing. Duckstaadt has shown (in *Reports from the Nile Delta*, for example) that he is a reliable, if conservative, informant. He may have overlooked a temple, and failed to notice a pyramid. But the Nile and sea are there, much as he described them. If Duckstaadt noticed it, it was there—though the converse may not be relied upon. One would not accuse him of imagination. Yet Alyse is a wife of the most scrupulous honesty, as any husband would demand. And the National Gallery of Our Patriotic Artistic Heritage is no laughing matter, least of all for a melancholic.

I remain bemused. Clearly, there is more to my wife's appearance than meets the eye.

'Do you think yourself pretty, Alyse?'

'Some might say so,' she reported, barely pausing for thought.

'And might those who thought so qualify the adjective with the modifier "very"—so designating you "very pretty"?'

'Some might' she claimed, not at all unpleased by herself.

'Despite the depredations of age and ravages of child-bearing?'

'Even so, Friedryk.'

'I did not know,' I conceded. For I was not told before. I'm not too proud to learn from my wife; though information normally flows down the gradient, in the reverse direction.

I feel like a nervous child, trusted with a dangerous burden, as when I carried my father's goose-gun. My wife is very pretty.

But I did not seek a pretty wife. Prettiness is the poor cousin of beauty. I fear the family connection. To my mind, beauty is overvalued—not half as pretty as she is painted.

Beauty is dangerous, the most heady of intoxicants, a pathogen.

It is a lethal metallic machine. It grips with claws of steel, expels all sense, and sucks a vacuum where once was reason. Beauty unhinges a mind, to expose quivering sensitivity. Then its swirling blades slice through the brain, like a mad surgeon's knife, leaving severed flesh to weep in its wake.

Beautiful women rarely care for science or scholarship. A crucial footnote for them might be as inconsequential as garter or silk bodice. They talk of sheen of their skin, or state of their chests, or vice versa, as if these were forces of nature—akin or rivalling magnetism or gravity. When they look to a man, they do not admire the lucidity of his prose, the elegance of his arguments, the reputation of his research. To these they are blind. They regard, instead, the superficial—the facade of his face, the cut of his waistcoat, style of his boots. If he is short, why then they think him slight. If he lacks the typical number of feet, then they brand him cripple. If he has reaped experience, then they slander him old.

Some regard a man as accessory, like parasol or cape, that must be matched to their colours and cut. Nay, less, for some would more readily cast off a man than dispense with a fur coat or fancy gown—even though he be Royal Academician and eminent biologist.

A woman afflicted by such an excess of beauty might even address this man as if he were spaniel or snipehund—some diverting, lesser form of life, provided by nature to yield brief amusements. Or, if retained as permanent pet, should walk to heel, lie upon her lap when she is bored, beg on his back feet for tid-bits. Were he to bark, it should be but briefly, so that she might laugh at his futile anger or impotent passions, before she despatches him to the kennels. If he rolls over to expose his speckled belly, why then she might tickle him. Quite.

I am prompted in these speculations by events of the 12th and 13th August 1876. I refer to Damascus and to Madame Hortense Virginie de Reve-Neuilly, to a reception at the French Consulate. From the flamboyance of her entry, the hushed awe she receives, it might be supposed that she, not Abd Al Kaddir, is guest of honour. It is a full hour before she thinks to notice me, many more minutes before she approaches to speak.

She is no linguist—her German execrable, her English poor. Since French lacks any significant scientific literatures, I have never sought to master it. I had long before abandoned any expectation that foreigners might learn our national language. We compromise with English. I make allowances, speak slowly and sound all vowels clearly.

'You are Count Freed-rick? The distinguished Count Freed-rick?' She nibbles her words delicately, as if sugar almonds, sucking appreciatively, closing her wide eyes gently in semblance of delight.

I explain that though well known, I am not fully famous. She finds this modesty *amusant*. Her golden hair is swept across, engulfing her right ear in a cascade of ringlets. To the side, her head seems afire with silver and amber lustres.

'I have read your works.' She fixes me unblinking with pale cornflower eyes, signalling some complicity whose depths I cannot fathom. The most unlikely persons are enthusiasts of Australasian mammals.

Her skin is pale as buttermilk but for the bloom of apricot upon her cheeks. The pert nose is sculpted to speak arrogant provocation. Her nostrils flare indecently.

'Of your *oeuvre*, Count, what do you value the most grandly?' Her face is shaped, exquisite, to an oval. The crimson wound of her mouth splits its swollen curves to disclose perfect porcelain teeth.

'The accounts of your travels are most...stimulating.' Her eyelids fall. Her lips purse to convey a sensual pleasure, or improper implication.

Her eyes are all knowing and all innocence. Stray strands of her hair nestle along the grove of her collar bone. Other tresses have slipped across the magic border of her dress, quivering to the pulse of her chest.

She leans herself so close upon me that my chin is all but resting upon the heaving slopes of her chest, which peek out from her bodice, blind innocents, new to the world. Betwixt and between the twin mounds, I see down the tropics of a dark interior.

Madame is of the unshakable conviction that I discovered the source of the Zymbasa. She will brook no denial. Having read accounts of the explorations, I am able to satisfy her curiosity—telling her of Lake Leopold XIV, the foibles of Spuck, the basking hippopotami, the pubertal rites of the local peoples.

Madame asks also of the erotic quirks of the Amazonians. She assumes I have personal experiences to quote. I am surprised that a lady might enquire. Again, a breadth of reading comes to my aid. I quoted some of the riper, if dubious, tales of Burton's. We discuss the curious paradox of the prodigious fertility amongst these female warriors pledged to chastity.

Some charming intimacy seems to have shrouded us like gauze from the surrounding company. I sniff at her neck and shoulders, gazing into the plump curves and intimate recesses of her ear. Her hand chances upon my wrist and lingers briefly. There is a rustle of dress and I feel her thigh pressed to mine, proximate to my groin, sending a shock of heat through to me. She speaks a time and address, then breaks away abruptly.

I feel hurt and perplexed by this sudden, chill departure. Then, I understand. As with many key discoveries, the answer pops suddenly to mind, as if sprung from a secret compartment. She means for me to come to her—at the time and place she has spoken.

Having detailed all this, fully and accurately, I see that the invitation was hers, as was the lamentable misunderstanding. It was never my intention to impersonate a libertine.

I encounter a state more naked than mere nudity, more revelatory, less clothed, more vulnerable.

Has man ever visited more beautiful places?

Freed from restraints, her hair tumbles down, coiling about her neck, writhing upon her chest, skimming about her shoulders and down her back. And there! The pretty valley, nobbled with spine, the secret dimple at the base of her back, the dents and furrows of red, bitten into her flesh by the discipline of clothes.

But, oh, the landscapes of her chest. What inclines, swells and swerves.

The soaring terrains stiffled breath; bring on the staggers. To see is to gasp, as though some hidden hand squeezes me by the gullet.

Fighting vertigo with each tenuous fingerhold, I descend, down to vale, around the cranny, through the plains, then the tussocked path, down to the depths of her.

I am torn down the ravenous precipice, through chasm, to gape, to yawning grove. How the crocus bloomed. And its heady fumes. The balms of her bounty. How essential her oils, musks of necessity, spice of her purpose.

What geometry. What proofs of passion. Did Euclid know such shapes could be made? And the rhetorics and refutations. Man soars, gravity suspends herself. Woman levitates and spins urgent somersaults.

What hot, wet refuge. How I am tossed and turned, and what harbour I find.

I must have passed out, succumbing to surfeit or exhaustion. For I wake to find Madame shaking my shoulder.

'Is Count Freed-rick ill?' But her tone speaks not concern, but, rather, some impatience or irritation.

'No, Madame, merely sleepy.'

'Sleepy?' she asks with surprise. 'Sleepy?' she says, this time with derision. One might suppose man had never slept with her before.

I turn away and close my eyes. I have never favoured pillow-talk. It is invariably inconsequential. When I wish to sleep, I am very determined. If I do not have my full seven hours, I am less than vigorous the subsequent day.

Madame has kept me awake well past my accustomed hour. She has received my best attention. But, quite insensitive to my needs, she persists in talking.

'Is this the man who writes such erotica? Who conquers Amazonians? Who discovers the Zymbasa? Whose conduct is infamy? The man they call the Tiger of Tunis?'

'No, Madame.' I grunt my defence. There is no call for her to insult me so.

She peers curiously down at my face, 'You are Count Freed-rick?' she teases.

'Yes.' Tiredness makes me terse.

'The infamous Count Friederick Bamburg-Minde?' Now I understand the curious twists and detours of her conversation. We are conversing with crossed purposes. She has mistaken me for a libertine.

'No. I am the famous Count Friedryk Baa MindeBerg. Without a hyphen to my name.'

Frankly, I am not prepared for the sharp change of her

manner. I thought my reply should reassure her. Minde is known to have hosted several contagions. He falls some distance short of being the gentleman. He is known to have formed improper liaisons with women, and led his wife a sorry dance. It is true his books are colourful, but at the expense of accuracy and rigour. Within the strictly scientific forum my work is the more highly regarded. I am a Royal Academician: he is not. I am a member of Bryke's Club, Minde had been widely black-balled. He is German: I belong to a peaceful and civilised nation.

If the lady's need were for conversation, she'd have been ill-advised to seek out Minde, who is the most morose and taciturn of men. All I have ever coaxed from him is a snarl, sandwiched between grunts. Beside him, I am garrulous as La Scala Chorus.

To be seen keeping the company of Minde would besmudge a lady's reputation. He might also compromise her health.

Her narrowed eyes bore through me with a look of some detestation. She sits up abruptly and seizes a sheet to her chest—pulling all covering from me. Why she chooses to clothe herself with such ironical modesty I cannot judge. For I have thoroughly surveyed all parts of her and know her uniform excellence. She is prompted first to moan, in short low bursts, then to release a extended warble in which she passes from soprano to contralto, then back again.

Of all the critical reviews I ever have received, this is the most immediate and hurtful—of being compared to Minde and found so wanting. Now I know how Hauser felt when, on its first night, his 'Fidelio' was compared so unfavourably to Beethoven's operetta.

As she claims, she grows more venomous. 'Pray, Count Ba-ba, if you did not discover Aafryka, what are you known for. I do not believe it is for your explorations in the bed-chamber.'

So I tell her to calm her. 'There are five scholars eminent in my field: Byrd-ffytch and Huxley in England. Schroeder in Berne, Kasselghuir in Cologne, Baa MindeBerg in Helikfors. I am the foremost.'

'Mar-zoo-phials?'

'Bandicoots and opossums, 'I say, 'wombats and kangaroos.' But this further confuses her. I am compelled to discourse briefly on their embryonic young and the mothers' abdominal pouches. I describe the Masupium itself.

'Pouches?' she speaks a sour and withering tone, 'I give my bed to a man who studies the bellies of animals?'

It is ever so. A familiar story. The layman does not grasp the imperatives of science, the logic of research. She is so far unconvinced as to push me roughly from the bed and refuse me readmittance. I see clearly that if I am to salvage anything from this deranged night and gain the rest I so dearly need, I shall have to decant myself to my own bed at the Pension Agaddyr.

Dressing rapidly, with all the dignity she allows me, I decide to leave her, to soothe herself and regret at leisure. She says little and reverts to French. It does not sound pleasant.

The next day I send her flowers and a copy of my latest book. She did not think it important to acknowledge receipt. It saddened me that we should part on such terms. For at the outset, we had been the best of comrades. And I never met such a body again, a perfection of flesh, exquisite as an orchid.

Whenever I consider the defining features of mammals, it is of Hortense's chest that I think. For I still retain a total recall of her thorax and abdomen, both.

So beauty charges her heavy price and extracts her interest through memory. Since then, whenever possible, I have evaded the predations and molestations of beautiful women.

Alkaloid

7th June

The scientific community will have supposed, from the paucity of references to my work in American publications, that I am not highly valued in the New World. But it is not so. By this morning's postal delivery, I received a bulky package from Chicago. Enclosed by a wadge of cotton lint was a letter and decoration. I have been awarded the Supreme Gold Lozenge of the American Zoological Association; on account of Sustained Service to Obscure Mammals. The letter informs me that the award is made 'First Class with Full Eulogy'. They address me as Professor. Either they assume I have been so valued by my own nation, else an Honorary Chair is attached to their award. I shall write by return to ascertain which is the case. It is unfortunate I am unable to travel to Chicago and meet there all my admirers and peers.

I wore my lozenge when I walked the park for pre-prandial exercise. It attracted the curiosity of children, envy of passers-by and barks from loitering dogs. For this is no ordinary, run-of-the-mill, decorative zoological lozenge, but a large gold-plated nickel slab, hung on orange and purple ribbon, from which dangle twelve gold-braided tassles. At a distance I might pass for Chief Councillor.

This unsuspected recognition had gone straight to my faculties, lodging in my capacities and energising thought. For I have just discerned an elegant solution to a problem that has long troubled me. It is of accurately calculating the speed of light; and, further, of ascertaining whether man or projectile might exceed it. If so, there would be difficulties—messenger or missile would arrive before they were despatched, delivering confusion and incredulity. Fortunately, this is not possible. All this is a side issue to my main studies, but the mathematics are intriguing. When I find some brief relief from the nagging summons of my science, I shall publish the proofs for they reveal quirky detail. I can show that the passage of time is relative to our speed of travel. At walking pace, this need not concern us. Yet frequent train travellers might gain an increment of life-span some minutes longer—all else being equal—and provided they did not suffer motion sickness nor dismount in Brussels.

But it is in the matter of Alyse that my researches prosper best. I have found a bridge across the chasm that separates science and marriage.

She had taken to bemusing me of late, revealing new facets, as though she were a discarded stone clutched up, suddenly swung into rotation to reveal itself a gem. The dazzle from her polished sides has left me blinking, with some presentiment of predicament. I had been thinking how I might best resolve the perplex. The solution has flashed through the fog like a shaft of sun.

My wife is a natural phenomenon. She is a particle of nature. There's nothing unnatural to Alyse. For she is a perfectly ordinary female member of that species of glabrous ape so densely populating Helikfors and its environs. As such, she must be as susceptible to scientific scrutiny and explanation as a crested grebe, anticyclone, vinegar beetle, quartz crystal or ferrous-oxide flake.

How sentimental and mystifying we become in our conceptions of our species! As though the god which guards our human realm were any more than the codes and laws of physics—awaiting full revelation. As if the soul of man were any more than the dance of his cerebral molecules.

When all is arranged, the marriage contract signed, the

marital sofa installed, the children conceived, born, christened, fed and placed abed, it must be conceded, as science asserts, that a wife is no more than the complex of her magnetic and chemical packages, bound tidily within the containment of a skin.

So I shall observe Alyse with that scrupulous rigour that is my hallmark. I shall devise hypotheses and match them to the data of her doings, test each for soundness to discern the theory that depicts her. If there can be laws regulating the dance of gases, there must as readily be Alyse-rules. She shall become transparent truth to my system. I shall have the facts. I insist upon them. A man internationally belozenged for his science of life will also know his wife. Else he is an idiot.

Initial propositions and observations:
    (a) let Alyse Baa MindeBerg = A (dependent variable)
    (b) let her change of state = $C = a - z$
    (c) such that $A(t_1) - A(t_2) = C(a-z)$
    (d) problem ascertaining the sum of (a–z) and their causes.

i. Alyse is changed (c), having become pretty, commenced laughing, ceased her melancholic abandon, become infected by confidence. She is more absent of home, forgetful of her domestic duties. A finds less pleasure than she used from our marital physiology.

ii. $a-z$ follow (chronologically, if not causally: the relationship might be a spurious coincidence) from my pharmacological research, her enthusiasm for Florentine painting, the company of Mr Aaskvist.

    (e) let my own person = B^{**}.

iii. $B^{**}(t_1) = B^{**}(t_2)$, i.e. I remain unchanged—being a constant: of consistently amiable and equable temperament, stable and disciplined habits.

iv. A constant does not evoke a sudden change. QED—A has changed independently of my influence (which is stable).

(f) let Mr Aaskvist = o

v. o has been in temporal and physical contact with A. They held hands and were seen smiling in the Gallery of our Patriotic Heritage.

vi. hand-holding and smiling are often—though not invariably—signals of affection.

vii. o must be held one possible causal agent of C.

viii. yet o is an inappropriate object of affection, he is also unappetising and stammers.

ix. A is an honest and decent dependent variable.

Question:
if $A (t_i) = A (t_2)$, yet $B^{**} (t_1) = B^{**} (t_2)$, does $o (A (t_1))$ yield: $A (t_2) = A (t_1) + C$?

if so, what of $A (t_3) = o (A (t_2))$?

might A change yet more?

x. I am temporarily hindered A and o are to make themselves unavailable for observation for two days. They are to go to Bernfors with o's sister Inge, for aesthetic experience. Their conjoint absence renders it impossible for me to continue to investigate my suspicions as to their relationship until their return.

And now to enjoy some alkaloid
Since Serturner first isolated morphine, many beneficial uses have been established. The substance has been termed 'God's Own Medicine' for its munificence—quietening the distraught, easing nasal congestion, stilling the persistent cough, arresting diarrhoea, dispelling headache, banishing insomnia, bursting the bubble of flatulence.

It is particularly efficacious for the young. The little ones are especially susceptible to its benign calming hand. I insisted Alyse dose the babies whenever they suffered wind. Even if they continued to burb it was never with any discomfort. An inner light of contentment would radiate through their pudgy pearly cheeks in a quite seraphic smile.

So kindly is this substance, doctors will not prescribe it before full diagnosis is made, lest all the symptoms scatter on the breeze of bliss. I know no clearer proof of the molecular theory—that mind and mood reflect the machinations of our molecules.

How I float down the gentle stream. How soft and warm the wind, how placid the waters. My senses so delicately sharp, I hear the squeaks of the voles in their burrows, smell the yeasty breath of cows, feel the tug of air as a swift swerves above.

And there is no pain. Gone is the persistent itch of an absent foot. No more is the crackle of wrapping paper, being tormented in my ear. Gone, too, the dull ache to my back.

From the meadows come the shrieks and chuckles of children at play. I raise my head to glimpse their games. Oh, those pretty girls with their tight fat plaits, the rustle of crinoline on creamy thighs, their dimpled knees, their wide unknowing eyes.

Come hither, child. Wriggle upon my lap. My soothing hand will stroke your hair. I shall blow a calming breath on the pink flush of your neck.

Some might think me odd. But I find nothing so touching, so melting, as innocence.

Memories are freed, unshackled of pains. I think calmly back to him, and also of he—back to that day in Chimba when Smugsen and I stand gazing down at the prostrate corpse of Oistermaa. The back of his head is crumpled as a cushion. The blunt instrument—a stone—lies glossy with gore, nestling aside his ear. He has been felled from behind by a single blow, and he has toppled like a tree. I doubt he sensed his attacker.

'Is he dead?' asks one of us. Neither wishes to examine the body for pulse or breath.

'He's as smashed as a breakfast egg.' replies the other.

But this did not answer the question.

'You found him so?' asks one of us.

'I came upon him just here.' says the other, 'It was not I that struck him.'

Smugsen and I sit some metres distant. Oistermaa completes our triangle. All three of us fall silent.

'What do we do with him?' Smugsen says at last, wearily, like a man contemplating a long journey. 'What do they do in Borneo?'

So we build a fire and smoke him, taking care that his head faces away from ours. It is not pleasant to gut a man. I am forced to do the work of two. Smugsen shows a queasiness that neither of us can afford.

We eat our first meal for two days, but neither can keep it down.

As the embers die, we bury our nakedness beneath the sands for warmth. There are two disembodied heads on the sands, and before them the feet of a corpse.

'What would we say, should we survive?' asks Smugsen. I feel he's lost his will, relying on me to answer for all his needs.

'We speak the truth. He saved both our lives. We came upon him dead from an ambush, killed by a savage hand. He did not suffer. We took care of his remains. His soul flew upward. What else might we say?'

And here is our dilemma, spread-eagled between us: a shadowed form, the face frozen to a scream. And here we are—three heads. The one posing the question, the other two to contrive an answer.

'Can we be forgiven?' asks Smugsen in a self-pitying moan, but not I, nor Oistermaa, nor God replies. We are abandoned in unknown wasteland and must chart this territory for ourselves.

A man's notions of God mature with years. And yet vary hugely with his circumstance. One might not think of his abstraction for months or years, till prompted by catastrophe to remembrance.

Now there is within me a taste for darkness that a diet of

reason cannot sate. Here in Chimba, I shiver uncertain. I fear some punitive hand might flick its finger to crush me like Oistermaa's cranium. This night I shall not be surprised by a pestilence of toads, inundations served with thunderbolts.

I know well enough that Saint Francis of Assisi, or the Archbishop of Helikfors, would not have done as I have. Measured by their exacting example, at least, I have committed grave wrongs. Yet I cling to the faith that God is a decent man and level-headed, who will make allowance for our desperate circumstances (and, perhaps, bear some small share of the responsibility for our plight). Above all, I am sustained by my conviction that different ethics must prevail in Chimba to those of Ludwig Prospect.

'Forgive us, Lord and spare us,' Smugsen moans. But all stays silent, save for the rustling of Oistermaa's hair in the whisper of a wind.

'Forgive me, Friedryk.' Smugsen abandons God and now makes his demands of me. Why ask that of me? Could I forgive? Was morality but a matter of manners?

'Silence! Sleep!' I instructed him, 'Soon there will be light.'

And with it come bald vultures, carrion hawks and gulley-crows, circling low above, shrieking, landing upon our burden, pecking and hacking at its surface, flapping their dusty wings, squeezing scaly talons, like dead men's fingers, deep into the flesh of him. And they look at us passionlessly with their sharp, cold eyes in their wizened, wrinkled heads, like a row of tetchy old men, shuffling along their humpbacked perch, as though we are their colleagues in carrion.

I have risked my soul for him. I will not easily part with him for importuning birds. So we trudge and fight, slash and shriek, squawk and scream for the possession of him. When tiredness and desperation overcome us, we bury the two pieces of him beneath the sand, slumped on guard. Rested, we disinter him, then shuffle on again.

Smugsen suffers the more—from the attentions and

wounds of birds, from a lack of proper sustaining appetite for our repast or task, from a wilting of his will.

So we rest for two days to build up strength from our diminishing and battered burden. He no longer resembles our friend. This eases our lot. Smugsen grows stronger. We cease to talk much. Grunt. Snarl. Scoff. Snort.

I realise, as Smugsen chews purposefully, eyes me distrustfully and stretches himself out in the better portion of shade, that only one of us may survive this trail.

Alkaloid (again)

8th June

Not even morphine can fully disperse my anger. Mr Aaskvist has no business borrowing my wife, even if he does take along his sister as chaperone. If he wants the company of a good woman, to take on excursion, to have conversations, to introduce to his relatives, to go picture-gazing of a Thursday in the Patriotic Gallery, why then he should procure his own, and pay for her, as I have done, by marrying. It is a quite improper and casual arrangement—using another man's—akin to renting an aunt or leasing a mother.

The example of those obscure American natives is most misleading. I refer to recent reports in the *Geographical Gazette* that certain Eskimaux Indians of Alaska loan their wives to visiting strangers—to chew the guest's moccasins (till the leather is soft enough for wear) to cook fish, and to engage them in sexual congress. They regard this as an increment of proper politeness. It is a very common courtesy.

I do not criticise these aboriginals. They have their reasons. Their culture has been shaped by a surfeit of snow. But their standards are not mine. For my part, I regard a wife as a very personal and private matter that should not be passed like a parcel nor used as a musical chair. Some might call me puritan, but such are my opinions.

They left me some hours ago, chattering with unnecessary loudness and jollity, clutching their hampers, easels, travelling rugs, flasks, bonnets, and sentimental novels. I stood in the hall as the door shut behind them, watching their silhouettes dance upon the frosted glass, sniffing Alyse's perfumes which hung heavy on the air. Evidently she showered in Eau de Cologne this morning, then doused herself in musk.

I feel rather cheated, to be frank. If my wife wishes to be exuberant and charming, why then she could rest at home and play the part with me. I have borne enough of her melancholy.

I cannot tolerate Mr Aaskvist's insolent, insubordinate manner. He is either aloof or, as this morning, insultingly familiar. Being gauche, he finds no more success when he tries to pursue the middle path.

'Is Academician Count Doctor Baa MindeBerg well?' he asked in a smug and predatory way, as a fox might survey a lemming. I explained politely that I had not grasped his gist. Did he suspect me of ill-health? Did I look as though I were ailing? I have always thought myself a robust and vigorous man—and no weakling host to stray infections. If he was not enquiring of my physical state, was he perhaps making some insinuation about my mind? Did he think me deranged, perchance?

He could tell that I was annoyed and that I had quite detected his rudeness. First he tried to bluster his way out, then he stammered an apology—all the time flushing pinker in a most unmanly gesture.

'So we are off to Bernfors by the sea,' he announced. 'Our train departs the Aalkmaa depot in three quarters of an hour.'

The effrontery of this quite drew my breath away. For within his remarks—so cunningly fashioned to a facade of pretty innocence—he cast his insults, then implied me the fool, thereafter hurling several imputations of ignorance.

A diligent husband would know, would he not, where his wife was going for an excursion? She would have asked his approval. He would have demanded to know the destination, purpose and duration of stay (Bernfors: Art: two

53

days). Was he implying I was too vague or haphazard to have made these proper enquiries? Did he suppose me a deficient husband who quite ignored his wife

The Geography lesson was frankly offensive. I do not think Bernfors obscure. It is well known to educated persons as one of the four largest towns of our nation. It is famous for its proximity to the sea. The marine vista offers one of the three sound reasons for visiting Bernfors. All this is known by most persons. It was certainly familiar to me. Why, even my tailor's dog—Fanii—knows Bernfors is by the sea. She frolics in the waves when her master takes her along on his jaunts to the races.

The Alkmaa Depot, I hazard, is also well known as the major railway station of our capital. The most occasional of travellers must recognise it as the terminus for the East Coast. I further suppose that even the most parochial of persons must know that the trains for Bernfors depart at eleven of the morning and three of the afternoon, on weekdays, and that having missed the former one needs must catch the latter.

'Really?' I said in a cold clipped tone, so maintaining my dignity in the face of provocation. 'Is that so?' But the irony was quite lost on him.

'And Bernfors is still by the sea?' I asked.

'So my map and informants tell me,' he replied, quite perplexed. 'And its residents believe so.'

I diagnose him one of those supercilious young men of limp mind who thinks others dull because they themselves decipher the wit directed at them. I am remindeed of Joshua Wengwe, my porter in Shamba, who upon viewing my meticulous scale drawing of an elephant pronounced it a pregnant mouse.

'Elephant.' I told him. 'El-ef-ant.

"No massa,' he chortled, 'him bugger too small. Him no sway big legs, no swish long snout, no crap him big turd. Him no side, no colour. This fella just symbol chappie. Squeak him for dead momma mouse walla.'

So it was casting science to Joshua Wengwe. And so it is

54

conversing with Mr Aaskvist.

I asked Mr Aaskvist if he had any plans to procure for himself a wife of his own. This was sufficiently bald, I felt, for a simple man to gain the gist. He reddened again, like a girl, and stammered that he thought himself too young and his prospects too uncertain. I concurred. It was pleasant for two such different men to find some meeting place of agreement.

As he left the room, I achieved a further diplomatic success with him. It was a deft and delicate gesture on my part, executed with a consummate precision. Clipping the inside of his left heel—it was the sheerest glance—I caused him to stumble, shed a shoe, then slide on his stockinged foot, scudding along the polished timbers in a quite comical manner. It was so droll as to force me to laugh out loud. He stammered an apology for his clumsiness.

Whatever may be said of his manners and physique, he does have a good head of hair. I saw this quite clearly as I stood over the tangle of him lying in the hall. The whole of his scalp is dressed in tight blond curls. Even on the crown, where many men suffer deficiency. There was no hint of pink flesh shining out from below. Perhaps Alyse is much taken of his hair. It strikes me as the only asset he has that I lack.

Since they left, I have examined my own cranium through a sequence of mirrors. I am not bald. That is just an appearance, a matter of mere perspective.

Being not absurdly tall, many can gaze down upon my scalp and view the central scarcity. Were I freakishly tall, like Hoosins, then I should seem the less bald, as he does, for none would then view my topmost parts—unless I was carrying company upon my shoulders or descending stairs before them. Baldness, then, is not so much an objective state of the subject, but a perspective, a certain perceptual stance of the viewer. Tall men are less bald. For they show their scalp not to the world at large, but merely to waiters, their wife and barber.

Yet I have made a discovery and ascertained a method.

The hair is thick to the two sides of my scalp. If I brush it up and over, the two growths almost meet. There is but a narrow strip of pink fallow to the centre. If I cultivated the sides, they might grow to embrace within weeks. Else I might grow on one side a thick curtain, to be swept over to cover the entirety of my naked crown. Then I should seem not baldish—but a hirsute man with a stylish and individual taste for a quite asymmetrical parting.

This plan pleases me as a further expression of my moral philosophy. We must each make the most of our talents and use to the utmost that which we have. As with my intellect, so with my hair.

I was thus pondering, sitting at Alyse's dressing table, brushing my hair with my left hand and clutching a vanity mirror in my right (to pass the reflection to the large mirror above the fireplace, and so gain the perspective of a taller man gazing down upon me) when Florynse entered the room. She did not think to knock; so giving me no warning, nor opportunity to discreetly remove Alyse's hair grips from my head.

'I came to make the mistress's bed,' she said, much embarrassed.

It is a well-known truth of society that when man and woman have not been intimate, yet find themselves alone together, in the presence of an unmade bed, then there is some unease. Each may wish to lie with the other, yet be uncertain of the other's desire. The poignancy is magnified, the potential made manifest, by the crumpled sheets, discarded underclothes, and perfumes of naked flesh. So it was we found ourselves.

'Stay, Florynse,' I told her, 'and talk with me awhile.' But she retreated towards the open door, stopping upon the hearth, holding her body stiff, evading the beckoning smile of my amiable eyes.

'I am fond of you Florynse. Though you are a servant and I the master. I an aristocrat and you a peasant. Though you are ignorant and I a scholar. Despite you being a girl and I a man. Notwithstanding all the differences in our stations,

56

I feel for you. I am fond of you, Florynse.' I paused to give her chance to reply. But she said naught, caught in a tremble of excitements. I could discern quivers to her shoulders.

'And I know you are fond of me, Florynse.' She was paralysed by her shyness so, as gentleman, I spoke the part for her. 'And I am a lonely man. My wife has left me for the charms of Bernfors. She prefers to paint by the seaside than rest at home with her spouse.'

In the transactions between man and woman, fraught as they are by the issue of gender, and prey to uncertainties and misunderstandings, one party must seize initiative. It is proper it be the man. Else nothing transpires. Time is wasted. All stays buttoned up. Tempers may fray. Frustrations ensue. So I dropped my trousers and freed myself of the undergarment, so revealing my full manliness.

'I shall go lie on the bed,' I explained, lest she miss my sociable purpose.

I know from my practical studies of women that they are often fey about quite unremarkable and natural portions of their persons, wearing unnecessary modesty—as if these parts were their own invention, rather than an inheritance, flesh on loan to them by nature, designed and repeated by history to enable the procreative act.

As a tactful man, I accept the pretence of novelty and defer to coyness. So I turned my back upon her and whistled a happy tune ('The Duke of Dorkmaa's Donkey') that she might undress without bearing my gaze, then slip unseen beneath the sheets.

It is a long, diverting song of five verses and choruses. I'd have thought she might have managed to unvest herself before I'd hummed to the end.

Yet when I turned to smile, to coax her in, I found myself alone.

Is she a stupid child, or does she seek to make me the fool? But she's a pretty girl, with those grey eyes, fine ear lobes, delicately sculpted ankles. I often think of her poor, fine feet, trapped in the bondage of her clumsy shoes.

This afternoon I shall go visit Mrs Vysinmaa's parlour.

It is most revealing. We have become intimates, book and I. I tell you all—because I trust you to hold my secrets with mute respect. I can recount to you those aspects of my life that I should not tell to man, woman or wife.

For each of us holds these secrets that we hide from others. We have consumed one friend, perhaps, and snuffed another, shot a bishop, ravished a sister, poisoned a botanist.

And we dare tell no person, for fear of their condemnation and the desertion of their affections. We are all so. Each of us in bondage to our past, which we suppose so shocking, encumbered by our secret, clutching the cold stone weight to our chest, bearing it wherever we go. And each of us is wearied and panting from the load. And each of us pretends we have no such burden, no gravid load tugged by conscience. This is our tragedy, that we do not share or spill our secrets, each man fearing his the worst.

Yet there is always one worse, and one worse still. I read but recently of that Hungarian gentleman who could gain erotic spasms only when witnessing the collision of railway locomotives. So he arranged such accidents, quite as his passions dictated. It is calculated that each of his ejaculations cost sixteen lives.

It makes a man glad he is no such pervert.

We tell each other stories, book and I. I commence and then you question me on the details of the matter.

Are you quite honest, Count Doctor Friedryk?—For you are sceptical and formal and will not bear any scribbled dross upon your crisp, clean pages. Is that exact and true?—you demand. And that adjective?—Do we require her services here? And in what order did these events transpire?—For you are rigorous and demanding. All must be spelled out for you. All i's dotted and t's crossed. You require I proceed from left to right, from top to bottom and over again.

You puncture pride. Do not succumb to the delusion that you are literature, Friedryk! We shall have no purple prose here. No congestion of syntax, no unworthy sentiment to sugar the tale. Lay bare the truth, you demand. Let us examine the gossamer details, before they are lost on the gusts of time, purloined by forgetfulness, swept beneath the carpet of mind.

So you speak to me, inviting me to read between your lines and glimpse—round corners—a hidden order. And in your true and sharp reflection, I face myself anew. Sometimes you are cruelly harsh, yet often strangely kind.

So you ate a man, Count Friedryk? How else would you have survived?

You suspect your wife? So you must, for the sake of you both. You are harsh to a guest? Nature did not fashion you to be a mat or doorstep.

It is reassuring to find my conduct cleaner than I first supposed.

Because I am a scientist and respect the lineaments of truth, and am freed of the flabby suppositions and sentimentality of the artist, because I write but the facts of the matter, and all of them, you document for me the order of my life.

It is fortunate I am an interesting man, else the exercise would quickly pall. Whatever may be said of me, I do repay close scrutiny.

I tell you this that you may make of it what you can. It is a dense opaque nugget and I cannot see through to its centre. Perhaps you can advise—

I have begun to weep to myself, violently and convulsively. And though I recognise no cause for sorrow, I am struck by the most abject melancholy. My face becomes bloated and crimson. The waters of my eyes moisten my collar. Deep furrows split my forehead. I heave, locked in spasm, as though wracked by a cough. It is as though my body has been borrowed for another's woes. And I have no inkling why I do it. It is embarrassing when Florynse finds me so, wailing at my desk.

'Has the master lost his whistle again?' she asks, 'or is his tea too cool?'

And I, the author of seven books and a hundred articles, Royal Academician, Chairman of the Geographical Institute, leading scientist of life, am patronised by the sympathy of a servant, as though I were some tearful child who had lost his rattle or fallen and grazed his knee.

I shall go visit Mrs Vysinmaa's. A man must have some leisure.

Ancrod

8th June

Where'er I've walked, death has stalked in my wake, skulking to heel, lurking dark in my shadow. He never fingered me, but often hugged my companions to his chill chest. Many I've known have died. It occurs to me that I am not lucky for my associates.

It was never my intention to shoot Gyorgy Moiklii-maastiirpi, who was both friend and Bishop of Peligfors. I had always been fond of him. I bore him no grudge. I never blamed him for the rudeness of his daughter Hanna when once peremptorily choking my preamble to a proposal. A man is responsible for his example—not for the use or neglect it attracts in others, even should they be his closest kin.

He was ever an amiable and genial man, good shot, keen sport, colourful raconteur, amateur of small mammals. If he had any evident personal fault, it was of falling asleep whilst talking to a man. Unlike others of his cloth, he was not forever boring company, trespassing upon their patience with hackneyed and unsubstantiated anecdotes concerning the sacred family. And he bore no puritan grudge against bosom or bottle, finding personal solace in both.

We each respected the other. He had a command of liturgy and scripture few might match, even should they strive to try. I was the young scholar—having already drawn attention to myself in the scientific forum with some elegant papers on Anura and Urodela. And Gyorgy, may he rest in peace, was a naturalist with a more than transient attachment to the badger. These being plantigrade cross between bear and weasel, digging for themselves obscure burrows which they defended with ferocity, he ventured that they reminded him of some ecclesiastical colleagues. For they are dogged, grumpy, eccentric beasts, trotting their solitary, repetitive paths bedecked in black and white.

Many a misty, rainy night I wander out with Gyorgy to collect fresh spraints and watch burrows. We sit alongside on the lower branch of an oak, watching silently for Brock, with no company but each other and our flasks of spirits.

And because we cannot talk, for fear of warning our quarry, there grows between us, in the dark of night, that fierce friendship possible between men—founded on shared adventure, warmed by the bottle, fed by companionable silence. Often, he will fall asleep on my shoulder, snuffling and grunting like the very animal we seek.

Our shared interest in wildlife manifests also in our passion for shooting game. Some oppose the slaughter of birds, arguing it a dull, damp, pedestrian pursuit, and the dead flesh rendered unpalatable by unpredictable grits of lead. But for myself, I always prefer to enjoy animals on foot than perched on a horse. There is more excitement, proximity to prey. Though nursery maids tell sucklings otherwise, though children read of hedgehogs in dinner jackets, though Gristvist's fables have it that voles transact philosophy with otters, life is a game of death. The Bishop knows this well enough when he ventures out to the field. He would not blame this truth upon man or beast. He accounts it to the divine design.

We are partying with the Buismans. It being the season, we gather to plunder snipe. I find my favoured position to the end of the line and further distance myself to one side. Here I can evade the glare when aiming, and can snipe those canny birds flying sideways from the beaters. And so comes a large cock, slow and low towards me, then rearing across to the left. He is a wise old bird—flying unperturbed an arc, level with the hedge to cover.

I know that I must have him—for his arrogant nonchalance, because I will not be bested by a complacent bird.

I swing, smooth as ball in socket, easing my barrel down to his height, following then overtaking his trajectory, assured I will draw blood this shot. There is a sharp tingle of excitement when one knows that one will kill. I pull as the point-sight alights on the chest of Gyorgy. He falls, just as the snipe passes behind him. It is a fine shot, and should have clutched the cock from the air, had a bishop not intervened himself (in sad and flagrant disregard of the protocol of the field).

When I come upon him, my dog is yelping in his ear with quite idiotic enthusiasm, frothing with excitement at the magnitude of our haul. He grips poor Gyorgy by his clerical collar, tugging in vain jerks, in his attempts to retrieve him. (The snipehund: this breed, it is well known, is congenital idiot. It does one thing well—it perseveres through brambles to clutch dead game in its mouth. It will apply this small fund of inherited truth upon whatever its master shoots. I have no doubt it would have deployed the same dumb tactic upon an elephant or moose.)

The bishop lies wide-eyed with an expression of small surprise. Here is a scorched weeping hole in his gullet. His crucifix has been buckled by the impact. Small beads of blood form upon his cheeks which are peppered by shot. (A shotgun wound: is always thus, of a forceful central thrust and a wide surround of scattered ball.)

His trousers are unbuttoned and drawn down his thighs. So has he dispositioned himself to answer an urgency of nature. Such are the contingencies and ironies of life, the whimsy of fate, that he is so shot—withdrawing from the kill, laying down his gun and urge to wound, to find some brief physiological relief. In the midst of life is death.

Yet Gyorgy would have understood—why the call from

his maker comes now, and in such facetious tone of voice. He was never perplexed in such matters. He was ever able to discern the designs of the divine hand in improbable places—fires, pestilence, locomotive disasters. I heard him explain his truths to the widow of a peasant who had been shredded in a rye thresher. He knew a good god. His god has called to claim him.

Myself, I am bemused and distraught. I tug his trousers up about his waist and button him up for posterity. It seems an important gesture and the least I can do to spare embarrassment—if not for him, whose concerns are no longer corporal, and beyond petty decorum, then at least for his survivors.

I am stretched on the rack of a moral dilemma. What should I do? For the best?

The decent, rosy-cheeked schoolboy within me pipes up that I should own up. This is a lamentable accident in which no blames can attach. A bishop, taken short, coyly seeking privacy, has been incautiously hasty enough to align his toilet with another man's gun.

But another voice counters the schoolboy. An urbane, steadier, authoritative voice—

'The least said, the soonest mended,' it advises.

'Thank you,' I reply. 'You speak wise counsel.'

Though it was not my fault, others might doubt. Suspicions would linger to taint my path through society. Suggestions of carelessness and unreliability would stick like burrs to my reputation. There would be whispers. When a man pots another man, invitations to dinner and the shoot quickly slow. I know this: Hoosins' cousin has suffered the fate. When a man bags a bishop, the stigma accrued is much compounded.

So I clutch Gyorgy up upon my back. He has the uncooperative gravid pull of dead flesh but, yet still warm, stays pliable. I carry him some hundred metres back behind the line of the shoot. If I am seen, then I can truthfully tell the tale in anguished voice. They can discount my erratic direction to my distress. If I pass undetected, then I can place him where the others have left. Where the beaters will shortly root him out.

I leave fate, or divine hand, to decide. They do not desert me as they had just abandoned a bishop. My reputation remains intact. Though the crack of guns sound loud, no eyes are cast back upon me. I hurry back to my former position. Having already claimed five birds, I promptly bag four more. It is uncanny. Some brilliance of vision and reaction seizes me. It is as though I can miss nothing this day. Mine is clearly the largest haul when our sport is abandoned at news of the tragedy behind our backs.

God knows, I am not a superstitious man. Yet it is clear to me that my life has been protected and guided by an unseen hand; a power independent of my will and talents, and yet stronger. Some hidden power propels us, to fortune or catastrophe, joy or misery. It has been most kind to me. This is the irrefutable lesson of my own experience. I am a protected person. For many times, in the company of others, I have floundered in utmost dangers, hurled down by the centrifuge of disaster—in Aafryka, on the fields of Peligfors, in the drawing rooms of society, in the bed chambers upstairs. And I have survived unscathed; save for the token loss of a single foot. And others have suffered or been snuffed out. Whilst bishops and botanists fall about me, I remain.

I believe that I have been touched by grace and saved for a purpose. I believe I have been saved to make my contribution. A man knows well enough that he is special.

Yet back to practical matters, and how best to observe a wife? For Alyse returns tomorrow with Mr Aaskvist, and I am resolved to have ready my instrumentation to receive them, calibrated to their conduct.

I know her as a faithful wife, devoted to my being—as should, indeed, be the case, for she swore a vow to that effect. And I support her; her dress-maker and milliner besides. I should be aggravated to find I was keeping another man's woman in hats. So I shall unravel and refute all evidence for suspicions.

A man cannot usefully watch his wife. To do so would transform the phenomenon to be examined. Observing her, I would see her watch me watching her ... which would render it a useless exercise. For I wish to see her candid, myself unseen. How to observe one's wife in one's absence? Now there's the conundrum that has teased husbands through the centuries.

I am prompted to professional practice. I pass through nature and observe. Were my wife a less reflective, self-conscious mammal—squirrel or sloth, perhaps—I should simply build a hide down wind, wrapping myself around in the ambient foliage. Could I conceal myself as household furniture or decoration, loiter behind the morocco spines of Bergmaa and Milkmaa, or recline within the piano? Indeed, I could not. It is too absurd and undignifed. A wife knows well enough when her husband is in the room.

Were she a bird, I should simply watch her flight from the balcony with binoculars—follow her soar and swoop, watch her clucking with her fledglings. But our capital offers so such vista, open as the skies. Its plan is not conducive. She need only turn a corner to procure some cheese and be quite lost to my view.

It is true that Alyse shows some features of a browsing herbivore, nibbling here, ambling then, trotting across some pasture to graze with some acquaintance. And yet I cannot stalk her. She would see me hobbling behind. Or else my pedal impediment might prevent me keeping pace.

So what does the methodology of science offer for the observation of a wife? She is a particular, peculiar case. For the observed herself observes. The hypothesis thinks for herself. You do not meet such problems with a magnet or a newt.

Further, I must catch her at those brief and critical moments (if, indeed, she has any). The most lewd of persons would not spend the whole day in turpitude, smiling, holding hands, wallowing in improper affection, whispering confidences beneath seascapes—or the enterprise would quickly tire. Rather, she would snatch such moments from her schedule of propriety, between a fitting at her dress-maker's, tea with an aunt, the matching of hats to her head.

So I must observe unobtrusively, at her critical moments, whilst she feels secure in her natural habitat. Experience informs me that this is bi-weekly, on the sofa, in the company of Aaskvist. To view her thus, I should have to enter quickly, without knock or warning, account plausibly for the abrupt interruption, to observe the qualities of their intercourse. It is a ploy one might use but once; and would cause the specimens to scatter in confusion, mistrustful of that place to reunite elsewhere. Should you so disturb courting grebes, you'd see nothing but the blur of iridescent wings.

No, I must be remote and find the higher ground. Above the drawing room there is a guest bedroom. I could bore a small hole through the boards, down through the ceiling below, then magnify—through glass and tubes—the sights and sounds beneath. There is a discarded hearing aid, a papier-mâché trumpet: and there is the four-inch reflector, I have trained on the lunar crevices. The holes would require some camouflage of cloth. I should need to move carefully above it in stockinged feet. Anouncing a change from habit, saying I was spending the afternoon at the Academy, slamming the door loudly to signal my departure, I should scurry around to the rear of the house, vault the wall, pass up the back stairs, undetected by servant or spouse.

The limiting factor is vision. I have made some experimental openings into my bedroom ceiling. Even with the guise of gauze, a hole exceeding a few centimetres becomes apparent. The distance between board and ceiling is slight, but a quarter metre, leaving a narrow tube for sight like the barrel of a telescope.

And there lies the answer! How readily can a truly rational mind effect an elegant solution.

Detaching the lenses for my telescope, and reversing them—placing eye-piece in the ceiling, and end-glass in the floor-board—I gain Zeus's Olympian view. The furniture shrinks and all is seen, curved over the convex floor, as though I were gazing through the eye of a cod, or perched in a ballroom.

There will be two adjacent holes, to admit sound and light. My remote eyes and ears, suspended upon the ceiling. I shall listen for their squeaks and watch them sport in their burrow.

I feel not unadmiring of myself to have so rapidly resolved this problem, finding the means to give my wife due attention. My faculties do not diminish or wither.

There remains time before my walk to sample today's pharmaceutical. Two drops of Ancrod—extract of viper venom—are said to do much to calm an over-nervous physiology. In extreme cases, it is documented, the drug may go so far

*

Events overtook me, causing me to miss my walk.

It was as though I had, in the space of but a single second, become encased in leaden armour. My limbs were quite numbed and, however forcefully I struggled, were unamenable to the merest movement, being quite impossibly heavy.

My face lagged, briefly mobile, and I was possessed of an itch to my nose of insufferable persistence. Yet my limbs being paralysed, I was thwarted in my urge to scratch. With the effort that might shunt a grand piano, I finally achieved a blink. This did nothing to alleviate the itch but seemed necessary to temporarily erase from sight the green and cream stripes of the wallpaper on which my eyes were inredeemably fixed. However, upon the closed lids of my eyes, the pattern of the paper cast its negative image.

One thinks little to the selection of a wallpaper until it is too late. A man might be so far negligent as to depute the choice entirely to his wife. Now I am forced to meet the cost. For, with my head immobile, and the wall stationary, I can see naught else but a circle of paper. It becomes my universe, and I quickly tire of it. After tedium comes irritation. It is thence a short time to torment.

The stripes commence politely enough, like the monologue of a bore. One has heard the story before, knows it to be long, but resolves to suffer the repeat. But these stripes turn malicious, twisting, bending, flickering, pulsing forward, then leaping back. It is like leaning over the side of a madly pitching boat. I am quickly nauseous and should enjoy a retch. But my tubes are too sluggardly to rise to the occasion. Yet worse than this discomfort is the remorseless naked persistence of the sight, as if these shapes of stripes are being etched upon my eyeballs in acid by a master of engraving. I should gladly relinquish my remaining foot to recover the capacity to blink.

But my mind tires even of this mischief and quite loses all focus to my eyes, till I am cocooned in a darkening sphere of opalescent green. I do keep my wits about me. I am still sufficiently attentive to note that something is amiss, and familiar enough wtih my own habits and physiology to quickly discern the deficit. I have ceased to breathe.

I am struck by the gravity of this, yet salvage some reassurance. Being paralysed, I have stopped breathing, yet—the compensation—being paralysed, I require less air. Further , if my respiration is the last funcion to succumb to the drug, it may shortly be the first to recover.

I seek some touchstone of time.

'Tick,' observes the clock. I think of Aafryka and Alyse, of my children and marsupials. I give some contemplation to my faithful monkey Benjamyn.

'Tock,' says the clock.

I count to twenty-seven before it sounds again.

'Tick,' it announces.

I am perched upon a tiny shaking ledge, above the abyss of infinity. And time, like the thin air on a mountain peak, is stretched by the sheer height.

That clock has struck some hundred times, like a distant

church sounding the hours. The minute lasts months. And through them I cling tenaciously to my tiny sill of life. There is nothing else to fill these weeks than to hold on, by the tenure of my finger-nails, and fight the pull of the chasm.

And peering down the hole of death, viewing the precipitous plunge of the curved and twisting walls, tightening with the depth, the sight reminds me of nothing so much (and I recognise it an unlikely simile, but biologists venture to unusual places) as the anus of a rhinoceros.

Then breath recommenced, the clock sped, my eyes tugged back to focus. I became aware of a wrenching to my shoulder and saw the face of Florynse, looming pink.

'Sir?' she wailed, 'Are you dead?' Logic has never been her strong suit. I should have reassured her that I was very much alive but my condition prevented movement or speech. Her face slid away from my sight. I heard the drumming of her feet on the boards and the crash of the door. I was alone with the stripes of the wallpaper which commenced again to dance.

Much time and swirling seemed to intervene before I heard the booming steps of Berthe, the cook, heaving her monumental frame toward me, like an aged bull elephant, and felt the gusts of her onion breath on my cheeks.

'Is he dead?' whimpered Florynse. Cook clutched my wrist, pushing her clammy, pudgy, pastry-pummelling fingers into me.

'The old bugger's none too perky,' she announced at length. Old? Bugger? I know but two meanings of the latter term. One more derogatory than the other. Neither apply to me.

The old crone then went so far as to tweak my ear, sinking sharp nails into the lobe, then jerking hard to prompt some reaction. I should have liked to reply but my condition quite prevented it.

'Mirror, Flo!' she instructed, revealing a rudimentary grasp of the science of life by embracing the empirical method. Notwithstanding the torments of experience and

70

my mounting anger at her rudeness, my face bore an expression of grave serenity, deep wisdom and much kindliness. The skin had turned a pale grey and my lips held a bluish tinge. Noble, immobile eyes regarded themselves unblinking. Slowly, small, milky beads of condensation formed a haze on the silvered surface, till they quite obscured the reflection of my mouth.

'The old coot's breathing, 'said cook, 'but he's none too sensible.' It must have been the relief, for they then both burst into laughter: cook cackling, then rattling her lungs in a bronchial.

'He's never too sensible, are you master?' she stared me full in the face, leering to show jagged brown teeth. Then she grabbed some loose flesh of my jowls and tugged it.

'Have a go, Flo!' she instructed. 'While you've got the chance. Why, you could pull his ears, or pinch his snout, bash his trotters or tweak his tail.' She reached out a blurred hand to my nose and tore a vagrant hair from a nostril. 'See,' she chortled, 'old coot don't mind. He's in a stupor again. Pig's been supping too long from his bottles.'

Florynse's face peered at me, first hesitant then defiant—staring at my steadfast dignity, she split her mouth and extruded the full luscious length of her pink tongue. I'm sure I quite grasped her gist.

Then a sharp point was poked—rude, hard and hurtful—into my buttock. Both laughed.

I cannot imagine what I have done to warrant the contempt of the servant class, but I pledge myself to revenge. But I am a patient mad. I shall bide my time.

Arachis Oil

9th June.

Alyse is returned to me having been on loan to Mr Aaskvist. Upon arrival she revealed herself in excellent spirits. There was a tremulous edge to her voice of husky excitement. The sea air had painted her cheeks with pink. The servants gathered around her, chattering their delight at her return and asking their instructions. They do not so readily comply with my desires.

It is as if the lights of the dwelling have been turned on after a long darkness. And I had not noticed the gloom.

Within hours, despite my sustained, concerned attention, she has wilted like a cut flower, hauling up a tarpaulin of morose melancholy to cover her former joy.

'Of course, I have been lonely without you, Alyse, yet if you enjoyed your excursion, and have the breath to inflate it to an adventure, I dare say my sacrifice was not wasted.'

'Indeed, Friedryk.'

'This reunion with your home and husband must give you delight.'

'Yes, Friedryk.'

'Your accommodation in Bernfors was adequate?'

'Yes, Friedryk.'

'You were given a good room for yourself? And you slept undisturbed?'

'Indeed yes, Friedryk.'

'And the company of Mr Aaskvist did not pall, despite his inanity, immaturity and unrelenting presence?'

'Mr Aaskvist was most companionable, Friedryk.'

'And you did not find you were mistaken for mother and son?'

'No, Friedryk.'

I had supposed that after two days' separation she would wish for my body in her bed that night, to consummate our reunion. I was mistaken. Alyse let me know, by the terse weariness of her tone, and her studied deafness to any intimate innuendo, that she would retire early and alone. She discoursed briefly on the great distances between Bernfors and Aalkmaa Depot, between Aalkmaa and home, and on the massive debilitations that travel can wreak on a frail person of the female gender. She quite capped this by proclaiming that sea airs induce exhaustion. It is a wonder sailors can keep awake.

A disinterested observer might have supposed from her tale that she was an invalid who had just swum home from Aafryka.

I question myself and examine my conduct. But I cannot resolve the enigma. I do not know what I have done to deserve a disdainful wife. It might be that my conversation is dull, being insufficiently attentive to bodices and bonnets. Perhaps I do not accord due attention to her left profile, which she feels the better of those two she has. It might be that an Academician of the Royal Society of Erudition, and Chairman of the Geographical Institute, is so far unintelligent as to bore the sharper wits of an advanced student of Hat-Purchase and Cake-Nibbling. Else it is simply that I lack a head of tight blond curls. If such is the case, it occurs to me that Alyse might have spared us both our matrimonial frustrations, by refusing my proposal and engaging herself instead to a sheep.

If I knew my fault, I might correct it and coax my way back to her affections. Perhaps I should simply ask her: 'Of my deficiencies and repugnancies of person, Alyse, which do you find the most offensive?' Then, by studying needlework, stammering, painting or blushing, I might become a proper husband.

'What have you done to deserve this?' my father would ask, cracking his riding crop on the polished mahogany flank of his cavalry boot. It was said of him (though never by me) that these glossy boots were the only reflective aspects of his person. This quite ignored his monocle, which would flash and wink to me, as if signalling an ironical commentary to his ponderous speech. Until I was thirteen, when I was briskly despatched to Naval School, he would see me by appointment on Friday afternoon review my conduct, then beat me with his riding crop.

There is no malice to him. He has few words and incomplete control of those. Talk perplexes him, forcing him to physical displays of his affections, through the instrument of his whip. Of those spirits within his care and control, I and his hunting mare Sophii are the nearest to the drawbridge at the castle of his heart. It was but we two that he spares the time to thrash, and with the very same crop.

'What have you done to deserve this?'

'Nothing, Poppa.'

He knows this is dishonest, and the placid marble strata of his face shudder, subside, then realign, under the weight of weary grievance.

'Boys are always brutes. If they say they are not, they add to their crimes by lying, and deserve to be beaten the harder. Boys are wild things. But with discipline, they can be moulded to gentlemen. That is why I thrash you, Friedryk.' And he pauses as some moisture disconcerts him in the corner of his eye. He is a straightforward man of unrelenting principle. He inherited his truths with his title. Both, he knows, will one day be mine. He is resolved to pass on both in good order.

'So tell me, Friedryk, why I should beat you.' And he aids recollection and confession by listing misdemeanours he thinks proper to my age and progress.

'Have you stolen apples?

'Did you take my duck-gun without permission?

'Have you been scoffing cider in the cellar?

'Did you steal my cigar butts and smoke them, Friedryk? Did they make you sick?

'You are growing to be a man, Friedryk. But you must not handle the milk maid. . . .'

It is thus I learn what is required of me to be his son and heir. He sees in me the dull refractions of his own dim childhood. I find some of his accusations offensive. Many are puerile. It's true that I've tickled trout. But I've never thought of affixing a cow bell to the verger. Frightening sheep and chasing milk maids seem pursuits for a dog, not a boy.

Yet I own up to please him and make him proud—that I am the proper son and he the good, stern father. It costs me little enough to please him. He is easily satisfied. Then he beats me. After, we shake hands as gentlemen, to show there is no ill-will—for he is father, I the son, and nature requires us to dance this pattern.

In return he awards me freedom and privacy. For he cannot exercise jurisdiction over those crimes he cannot conceive. I am free to wander beyond the perimeters of his imagination. It is a wide and open country.

I teach myself Latin to enjoy the salacious poems of Catullus. I have spoken Our Lord's Prayer backward at midnight, to summon the Prince of Darkness (who never comes at such late hour). From my early studies of Chemistry I have learned to construct bombs to explode some cows, and have built a still to yield pure spirit. Fires do interest me. It is a compound pleasure: I enjoy the soaring flames and seering heat, the frenzy it begets in others, the lingering after-glow of my handiwork. I started first on hedges, and have progressed to cottages via hayricks.

I do not molest the dairy maid. She has the broad flat face of a barn owl and reeks of rancid butter. Instead, I learn some rudiments of eroticism with my sister Siigrid, whose face has the delicate features of a procelain doll, whose surfaces smell of sandalwood and rose-water, and whose recesses much intrigue me.

I gain some wide self-education in the yawning spaces my family allow me.

I shall hear no ill said of mother.

I developed early an interest in natural history. The natural quite naturally interested me. I was fully conversant with my intimate parts and had often seen the larger, hairy, grotesque parodies of these that my father wore in the steam bath. I sympathised with him in his deformity, supposing that he had been born sporting some disfiguring lumps or had suffered some inflammatory infection.

I was much confused around the age of five. In a household of mother, two elder sisters, three aunts, maids, nanny and cook, the example was primarily female. Father, of course, was the exception. He was always the exception, like a reindeer stumbling in dazed upon a human encampment.

He seemed one of those singular things—like stove, sauna, dog-cart, dining table—of which each household had but one, to render it complete. And like these, he seemed a functional item (though I had not discerned his use), to which one might turn occasionally. One needed a bath but weekly—though cleanliness ranked high—why use a father more often? And he was usually quite silent as a fixture, emitting low growls as the pressure of gas guilt up—glimpsed smoking in the library, belching like a stove, or sliding silently down corridors, like a dog-cart moving distant along a lane. In short, he seemed quite incidental to our human and social life. He was our domestic equestrian statue: monument to some serious adult concern, long past. Solid and prepossessing, yes: but beyond my ken, and insufficiently animate or immediate to provoke much curiosity.

Naturally, then, persons being female and older, I formed the theory that boyhood was a transient phase through which all must pass before they could mature to be

76

a woman. So I knew that, sooner or later, I should transmute to a female, as surely as the grub grows to butterfly. I had some vague presentiment that this would involve the loss, or change, of that thing between my legs. No matter, it was only good for micturation. Its sacrifice seemed a slight price to pay in order to wear fine dresses, grow my hair in long lustrous tresses, rouge my cheeks, play the piano, and be fully admitted to the intercourse of the house. For I had grown to resent the way they would scowl, hush or change the subject, whenever I barged into a room.

'Nanny Bergstaadt, when shall I grow to be a girl?'

'When pigs sprout wings,' she advises. It is distressing to find one's fate tied in with the beasts of the sty. And it strikes me as a poor career. For I know the squeals of slaughter at Christmas. A festive day for people is a sorry time for pigs.

'Tippi, when shall I grow to be a girl?'

'When you are quite good enough,' says my older sister, with malicious relish. So has wickedness stunted my growth?

'Siggi, when shall I become a girl?'

'Don't be silly, you've got a villii.'

'But it's not my fault,' I protest.

'Are you sure? You did pull my pigtails.'

'I had it before then,' I say scornfully. For I have acquired an early scepticism.

'Mamma, when shall I grow to become a girl?'

'But you shan't Friedii. You are Mamma's little man.' And she holds me firm as I sob my sorrow and roar my rage.

'But it is better to be a man. And when you are old, you shall be a Count.' This strikes me as poor consolation, having seen the example of my father—proud and mad as a billy-goat, spewing smoke, drinking alone in the library, watching the world with bleary and mute distaste.

Time passed. I learned the general principle of gender. It

must have been six or seven more years before Siigrid and I discussed the matter again. My thoughts by then had reversed. I now saw my member as a natural extension. My curiosity was in finding what women had in its stead. I had closely regarded the rears of sheep and cows. But they gave distorted, unlikely cues. Women, I knew, were otherwise.

'You cannot see my whatsit,' Siggi announces one day in the garden, apropos of nothing, 'For I shan't show you. Mamma says down below is very private.'

'You've got no villii.' I taunt her.

'Should hope not, too. What would I do with one of those. They're really quite inelegant.'

'You can't pee standing up,' I add with derision, thereby exhausting my small fund of knowledge.

'Shouldn't want to. It's vulgar.'

'So what have you got instead?'

'It's not instead. It's better.'

'What?'

'Shan't show you ...' she pauses to consider, 'or if I did you musn't touch it.'

And stooping below the umbrella of weeping willow, leading me by the hand, she squats in the shade. I hear the rustle of skirts of muslin being drawn up to her waist. My eyes adjust to the gloom. And I see. My first surprise is its colour.

'Girls have pink knickers,' I observe, as if I'd known already.

'There!' she clutches her lace-edged hems and displays the creamy flats of her thighs. 'My legs are very lovely,' she says, 'that's why I'm showing you.'

The air is heavy and warm with pine resin, the crickets sound their insistent rhythm, and her legs are strangely lovely. I feel a compulsion to fondle her thighs and run my hand to the edge of her pants. She is smooth. Some of her is cool and other parts are hot. She twitches to the touch.

At first I think there is nothing there. This is a superficial judgement. She has swollen satin curves, plump pink folds and a secret place.

'You can touch, then,' says Siggi, soberly watching my meandering hand. 'But no more.'

'Don't be silly,' I say. 'What more is there.' But then remembering the animals, I put one and one together.

How pretty they were, those days of innocence with Siggi. We were a family together, before I was suddenly cast from the garden. They sent me to Naval School to learn discipline amongst men.

Arachis oil? I suspect a typographical error—Brachis? Arichis?—or else a facetious author. These things happen. We wasted much time trying to replicate Grimaa's Phenomenon till we realised he was quite mad, believing himself a cormorant (he would squawk at students and push raw herring in their ears, as if feeding his fledglings).

Helmsburg had much malicious fun in creating two imaginary Hairy Tree Toads, entering them in his *Lexicon of Amphibia* and attributing them to North Aafryka. He was forced to concede his creative crime. But the admission came too late to save poor Hoosins from embarrassment. For the credulous fellow had by then already published his treatise on the unlikely reproductive practices of these fictional toads. I did not laugh or condemn him, he being my friend.

They'll not catch me out so easily. Arachis oil, indeed? And what good is that, pray? One might fry one's fish in it, but I'd hoped for rather more.

It is a yellow viscous oil, compounded from crushed peanuts. I have tried all approaches to intoxication; all to no avail. Why, I have drunk it to sickening excess, smeared it on all my mucous membranes, inhaled its vapours, smoked it on the end of a cigar. It does nothing to interest a man's mood or perception. It leaves stubborn stains, on his collar, cuffs, and underwear.

Baamii's Assuagent

11th June

At least I have my science. I shall document the occurrences objectively. I shall observe total fidelity (how I wish that the same could be said of my wife).

I shall make a scrupulous record. Conclusions derive from an adequate appraisal of the full data. Damn her. I shall deploy the full armoury of my method and system. The hussy.

Am I a toad *(Bufo)* (Baa MindeBerg) (to count so little)? Even were I, what of the rights of a toad? May he not reasonably (I leave aside any considerations of (axiological) morality (and appeal instead to probability (for the pig may be fed each morning from the gentle coaxing hand of the farmer's wife for three hundred and sixty-four days in succession (but it does not mean it will be fed on the morrow (It being a leap year) (for it will be promptly cut and bled (for it is Christmas Eve (and has been fattened to be eaten by the farmer's family (and relatives) who will chortle and guzzle (as the grease runs down their chins))))))))(this toad (before cited)) expect more than to be trodden underfoot and smeared (its viscera spewing through its split underbelly) to become a repugnant, twitching eyesore (how fastidious their vision) to persons passing by? (!)

How low am I sunk! How low am I sunk? How once I soared.

Am I so deficient as a husband (this being a relational term invoking the corresponding category (wife) (to which attach corollary obligations (of respect (certainly (albeit there is friction (in which a man may be so grievously angered as to display an unattractive facet)) and fidelity (absolute (mental and physical)))))) to deserve this (and there was indubitably more (and more to come (?)))?

Yet, is this a problem of logic? And if so, do I have the mental strengths to resolve it? I feel weak and my engine is stuttering.

By what computation and derision of vulgar faction can she so diminish my number?

I shall gather some bottles and broach them to float this problem.

Be calm, Friedryk. Describe dispassionately.

I reached my hide early without being myself observed. Having scampered across the back garden, I heard Florynse and Berthe in sufficient time to secrete myself in the cupboard at the base of the stairs. They kept me imprisoned there for several minutes. For they loitered near the door and held a seminar—though they reached no definitive conclusion—upon the relative hardness and pungency of three cheeses, the fragrancies of their mistress's soaps. It did not escape me that I was paying for them to engage in this colloquoy. They then found themselves sufficiently tired by this domestic labour to declare themselves deserving of a rest. So they retired to the kitchen for tea—so enabling me to slip up the stairs to the first floor.

I spied Alyse alone in the drawing room, where I tethered her after lunch. She paced about in a relentless figure of eight, circling a path around sofa and piano. (Note: the subject appeared agitated, quite unlike her lethargic self at feeding time when her appetite was depressed and she barely vocalised.)

The sound of our front-door bell seemed to heighten her anxiety. She stopped abruptly as though startled, then pedestrated to the mirror. I then observed her to engage in a variety of auto-tactile behaviours: manually adjusting her occipital hairs; rotating her cranium through one hundred and eighty degrees whilst patting her cheeks and pursing her lips; running the palms of her hands down her torso and hips. She seemed reassured to have retained all those portions of herself that she remembered last having. Such self-grooming patterns are common enough throughout the mammalia, so it may be a mistake to endow them with undue significance or see in them the application of any high intelligence.

Florynse knocked at the door. Alyse invited her entry. Florynse announced Mr Aaskvist. Madame invited Florynse to invite Mr Aaskvist to join her. These transactions were successfully concluded in the appearance of Mr Aaskvist and the prompt departure of Florynse.

Male and female stood stationary and apart, occupied in mutual regard. This is a customary pattern when a mature male mammal is admitted to the cage or territory of an adult female. Though cosmetics suppliers argue otherwise, smell is relatively unimportant amongst the humanoids. Dogs, for example, would have proceeded from this mutual observation to a tentative and cautious sniffing of the other's genital regions.

Instead, such is the conceptual complexity of our species, Mr Aaskvist posed a question (albeit a rudimentary one):
'Is he here?'

'He is not,' replied the female—causing the male to smile—'He has gone to instruct the Royal Academy.'

'Then I shall have (?) you upon the floor, five times.' observed the male. The acoustics were less than ideally resonant, and his stuttering speech and lack of confidence rendered it difficult catch all of his vocalisations.

'Be serious, Modyst, my dear.' The female admonished. He advanced upon her, stopping only when separated by centimetres. The two being of corresponding height, they thus looked full-frontally into each other's eyes. She leaned forward to plant her fleshy peri-oral tissues upon his, then promptly detached them. He reached out his upper limbs to hold her around the lumbar region, such that their faces were again shunted together. This was sustained for the best part of a minute. Both rotated their heads through some few degrees in synchrony. They swayed somewhat yet still managed to maintain themselves in the vertical.

There was a reddening of their facial tissues. This was more pronounced in the female whose cheek pouches were particularly touched. Throughout this, they must have been breathing through their noses.

I should not wish to succumb to the anthropomorphic fallacy, but I concluded that they were 'kissing'.

Briefly tiring of this, they then sat upon the sofa, buttocks resting on the cushion, the soles of their feet upon the floor, in the characteristic Sapiens leisure-posture.

'He suspects?' asked the male, rotating his torso, extending an arm to rhythmically handle her patella.

'My husband suspects that bats and newts have common ancestry, that carpets are deleterious to human health, but he shows no signs of applying his intelligence to the condition of his wife.' I recognised the tone as that commonly designated 'sarcasm'.

'He doesn't like me,' the male observed.

'Nor should he, Modyst. You are a naughty boy.'

There was further bi-oral behaviour and heavy nasal breathing. The male reached up a hand to contact the left mammillary swelling of the female's chest. She seemed oblivious or accepting of this. He was perseverant in attending this part, engaging in some circular stroking and light clutching before inserting the digit of the hand into a vent between some buttons of her blouse. Fumbling behaviour was apparent before the gap was sufficiently widened to allow full insertion of the hand. There were

83

some shivers evident, and low-pitched vocalisations, from the recipient of the fingers. Her thighs jerked and then spread limp. The male evidently discerned this without looking, for he shortly detached the hand from thoracic manipulation to engage in upper femoral stroking. His mouth was lowered to the female's chest to display pseudo-infantilist-feeding-reflexes.

The male's mobile hand (the other was stationary about her back at the level of the sacral vertebrae) ventured against the restrictions of garments. Having reached the patella, it was inserted below the female's dress and commenced an upward path beneath, reanimating her thighs. Its progress having been evident as a bulge below the cloth along her thigh, was then concealed as it was lowered to the interfemoral space.

The sound of Florynse in the passage clearing her bronchial tracts had a quite pronounced effect upon the pair. Both exhibited a strong startle response. They sprang up and apart, ceasing all manual contact.

Despite her presence in the corridor, Florynse took a further minute to knock at the door. She brought them tea, it being three of the afternoon.

'Do you have rats, Alyse?' asked Aaskvist.

'I should think not. Why should you ask?'

'I thought I heard one, scratching above in the ceiling.'

Rats, indeed. But I thought it wise to leave the hide.

Belladonna

12th June

For the moment, I shall clothe myself with the dignity of silence. There are several issues to be resolved—my honour, the moral climate of my household, the lewd misconduct of my strumpet wife. Above all these, paramount and ever foremost in my mind, is the welfare of my dearest children. Bless them, the innocents.

I am not a man to be crossed. I make an unfortunate enemy. Though it is true I am never vindictive, I do defend myself against wanton attack with fierce resolve, deploying the unrelenting cold focus of a special intellect. Smugsen learned this just before he died.

'Good morning, Friedryk,' spoke the fallen woman. She was brazen enough to smile. I held a steadfast gaze ahead, evading the libertine's face, and passed mute along the corridor, so maintaining decorum despite her insufferable provocation.

No, it is not a good morning when a man discovers his wife a harlot.

We conversed no more until breakfast time.

'Are you quite well, Friedryk?' the trollop enquired. She was sufficiently adept at the Thespian Art to convey an illusion of concern.

No, Alyse, I am not well. I have learned that my floosie wife unwraps herself for the hands of passing strangers. It makes me quite upset.

Fortunately, I retained sufficient discipline to stifle a

welling outrage. I kept my dignity, laying it snug by my silence.

'Are you drunk, Friedryk? At nine in the morning!' I swear my wife went so far as to imply some criticism. Of me. In the circumstances, I found her irony ill-timed. I had not intended to bestow her with my regard. But I could not resist casting her one glance. She turned scarlet and spoke no more. Evidently, she'd gained some taste of the flavours of my feelings.

'What have I done, husband,' her silence pleaded.

You know,' roared my hush.

'Whore,' spluttered the gagged voice of decency.

'So you have found me out? You know the depths of my squalid debauchery?' came the echoing sobs of her voiceless shame. And she rushed from the room, slamming closed the door on her abject humiliation.

I felt much heartened, ate some cheese and two more eggs. Then I lingered over coffee. This was but the first salvo in an unrelenting hostility. But I was satisfied enough. I'd acquitted myself well, with serene dignity, and had won the first skirmish. I think I shall force down her face till she sinks in the mire of her degeneracy. First, I shall continue my studies. I cannnot allow her to so disturb my equilibrium.

Belladonna calms the pulse and breath. It really soothes a man. It is a fortunate coincidence of my needs and science. My eyes do stare somewhat—piercing pupils in lakes of white—but this is a characteristic effect of intoxication.

'We are blood-brothers now,' says Bertii Smugsen, 'cannibals together.' He has taken to such excesses of speech, moving by turns through loud wails of unproductive guilt ('Forgive us Lord. Spare our souls. We are the most depraved of sinners'), cloying, unreciprocated and improbable pledges of affection ('We shall never be parted, Friedii, you and I') and risible para-philosophical observations ('The world, Friedii, is like a ripe apple with a maggot eating its way out from the core.').

My naked skin is cracked and bleeding from the fierce, unblinking sun. A dry purple swollen tongue clogs my mouth. My bowels ache from a meagre ration of rotting meat. On my back I carry a human torso, its broken ribs piercing my shoulders. And my feet are broken open. As if these discomforts are not enough, there is the conversation of Smugsen. During the day we tread an unsteady gasping path over undulating dunes. This quietens him. But with the night-time fire throwing menacing patterns on the black terrain, he grows quite garrulous.

Without a mite of encouragement, he has proposed and then supposed for us some mystical union—that our lives are inseparably joined, that hereafter we should labour for the other's welfare, in sickness and in health, for better and for worse, forsaking all others. He extends this principle to our property. But I did not wish to marry him.

'Have you finished with that bone, Friedii? Really?' And he sucks the ivory surface then cracks and crunches it. 'I do not have much at home. But what I have is yours.... And your family's estate at Bergmaa? Tell me of that, Friedii.'

I do not think myself mistaken in suspecting a concealed threat of blackmail.

'Umm.' He snaps open the bone and licks at its centre. 'No one must know of what we have done, Friedii. You agree? We must build our lives anew.... A man's life is like a slate on which others write. We must protect ourselves from slanderous scrawls.'

He further opines, with some originality, that Aafryka is a long black tunnel; that our King is a distant star, twinkling his grandeur; that love is the cement holding the bricks in the house of society; that our families are pomegranate seeds.... He proposes that our friendship is the sun on the leaves of a silver birch after long, cruel winter. It occurs to me that he will be the tree, and I the generous element.

I bid him to silence but he takes little notice. Or when he does, he addresses instead the tattered remains of Oistermaa which I find yet more disturbing.

It strikes me that, in Chimba and hereafter, I shall be the better without him. The same observation holds for my depraved wife. I think I shall dis-marry.

The dissolute one addressed me over the lunch table when Florynse had served the fish. I do enjoy a cod that has been fried in black butter. Berthe had prepared with it mashed turnip, kale and beetroot gravy: I think she sought to give me a treat.

'Friedryk...' the tumbled woman began, and gave me the pained baleful gaze she might bestow on a child in tantrum, 'you clearly have some grievance.... Perhaps, you should disclose it.... You are upset.... It may be you think I've slighted you. So speak your mind. Then I may answer and we might easily resolve the supposed offence.... Were your boots not polished properly this morning? Or was your coffee too sweet?'

But I could not accept the axioms on which her speech was built. Firstly, there was the arrogance of her mode of address. She spoke to me as an equal, and an innocent at that. Whereas her conduct had quite lost her a husband's respect. She had fallen and I would not deign to lower myself to her pit. Her implication that she was the injured party was so disingenuously offensive as to cause me to flush with anger.

I do not suppose manual and oral adultery to be slight matters that can be facilely resolved. They amount to domestic treason.

'Well, Friedryk?' she sustained her pose as a reasonable and civilised person.

Of course, I neither looked at her nor replied. She reminded me of that murderer who returned the same day to the scene of the crime, requesting of the grieving widow the return of an umbrella he had left behind. I am ever bemused at the infinite capacity of persons to explain away their conduct or cloak it in reason.

'I am only your partner,' continued the aggrieved, abused party, 'but it seems to me you might answer. Instead of acting the infant.'

Needless to say (so I did not) I found the analogy of myself as child to be partial and distorted. Evidently, she sought to wrong-foot me. She caused me to recollect that Hungarian who, having slaughtered a hundred souls by arranging collisions of trains, wailed that the prosecuting attorney was disrespectful.

I continued to dissect my fish. The belladonna keeps me wonderfully calm and clear-headed. When Florynse returned I had bade her bring another bottle of wine. My calm, reasoned and polite tones in so doing established to all that I was behaving with scrupulous propriety.

This quite cracked Alyse's composure, for she then resorted to infantile gambits.

'Perhaps my husband is going deaf,' she observed to herself 'or has succumbed to senile decay.'

No, Alyse. My ears are sound, my eyes are sharp, my mind fast and lucid. I heard, I saw, I reached my irrefutable conclusion. My wife is a pervert; a shameless strumpet.

'You are not going to answer me, Friedryk?'

This was obviously a trap. And a very cunning one too. But she would not catch me out so easily, for if I answered 'yes' or 'no' I should have to contradict myself, be tautologous or unclear—speaking that I should not speak or commissioning a double negation, so render myself ambiguous. So I said nothing, which had been my intention, but forced myself unwillingly into a mute affirmation. It suddenly occurred to me that the hussy might have spent her morning reading philosophy in an attempt to so disconcert me. Perhaps I had under-gauged my adversary's wiles as I had underestimated her depravity.

Smugsen and I have been thirteen days in our plight; though time seems an endless strip in which dots of sleep punctuate the tortured trudge of our split feet over scalding sand. We are not even sure if our line is straight, or where it will lead us. But I tramp ahead, he following, sustained by the faith that our path will eventually be broken—by some renewing stream, by foliage and food, or by some human settlement. And so it is.

The sun has not fully risen when we catch the acrid smell of smoke, then see its drift, diffused by distance.

'After our long penance, the Lord saves us,' shrieks Smugsen, dancing a wild jig, then embracing me and planting the dry hide of his lips upon my flaking cheeks. 'See, Friedii,' he gurgles his joy, 'life is like an umbrella which....'

'Shh.' I say. We should proceed with caution, find out who it is that lies ahead, prepare ourselves. First we should bury the lingering remains of Oistermaa and pay our last respects.

'They might be cannibals,' I tell Smugsen, who pales at this possibility, 'this is a land of wild peoples.'

'Friedii, friend,' he tugs at my shoulder and his eyes stare wild, 'we must never forget our pact.'

We scrape with clawing fingers a shallow hole for the third party, and lay to rest our secret burden of his pieces. Smugsen says some words and wipes at the moist salt smudges on his cheeks.

'We must keep our pact,' he repeats, 'we must protect each other. If either tells, the other is lost.'

Quite oblivious of the contradiction, the garrulous man then bleats of his discretion. And with my estates and his acumen, he proposes, we shall prosper well together. When we both reach home.

I am not a man to be threatened.

'If you do not cease your absurd silence, I shall not answer for the consequences,' said the courtesan as we finished our quiet supper together. 'A wife's patience may get strained.'

I could not help but admire her brazen confidence as she threw down the gauntlet and challenged me to combat. There was some touching absurdity in her belief that she could threaten me, in a contest of morality, defending a lost position. It was like having a lap-dog snarling at one's ankles, or a child shaking a pudgy fist.

Dissolute and depraved she may be, but she also shows some pluck.

Biedermaa's Unction

There was a strange man in my bath this morning. But first to the pressing matter.

I had braced myself to confront Alyse today, state my irrefutable case against her, then arrange the dissolution of our fractured union.

I knew myself quite justified in tearing, shredding then burning, her new collection of dresses. Some might think it wasteful. But the pleasures thus afforded far outweighed any costs. It is a well-established ethic of our culture: what a man pays for is his to dispense with.

'Countess Baa MindeBerg,' I had thought to begin, 'You have fortified your right to the name. Henceforth, I shall call you 'you'. To address you as Alyse would imply an intimacy that I no longer wish to sustain.' I should then pause until her shocked sobs subsided.

'Two days ago,' I would continue, 'you shamed me. You shamed yourself, so severing our partnership. You entertained Mr Aaskvist. I'm sure he quite enjoyed you. Mouths were placed together. One such incident might be forgiven, and with difficulty forgotten. But this was sixteen times, for a total duration of thirty-nine minutes. hands touched portions of your person—I shall not name them—which a good and proper wife reserves for her husband, and would only otherwise reveal to a doctor or midwife. And I know of no medical practitioner who would conduct such oral examinations.

'In these circumstances . . .' I would then have drawn this

91

to its inevitable conclusion, 'you leave us no alternative but to separate.'

I would be quite unmoved by her abject pleas, wails, howls and related observations.

'Those who framed the marriage laws of our nation did not have the imagination to anticipate women of your depravity. If we cannot divorce with dignity we shall firmly and finally separate. I will make you an allowance though less than you currently gain. There should be no sacrifice. Mr Aaskvist will wish to buy you a wealth of clothes, support your milliner, and ensure a sufficient supply of maids.'

I do not see why I should continue to pay one hundred and twenty ffenyngs a month just for one adulterer to enjoy the hats of another.

'You shall have regular access to your children so long as you consent to the constant supervision of a nurse. I cannot allow the risk of moral infection....'

I had scripted all this carefully in my mind, as tidily as I might have prepared a paper for the Academy. Why, I'd even anticipated questions, and had steeled myself against emotional appeals and irrational arguments.

It had to be said. But the enormity of it held me temporarily in check.

So we had another silent breakfast. But, today, the woman seemed not a mite disconcerted by my taciturn tactic. I allowed her time to prepare herself to face the perils of her position. By half an hour past eleven, I had fully braced myself. I summoned Florynse and despatched her with a letter to her mistress.

I shall speak to you now.
 F. B. MB.

For some inexplicable reason, Alyse being in an adjacent chamber, the reply was thirty minutes coming. Florynse delivered it with quite inappropriate good humour. I suspected her of amusement.

I am in the living-room.
A.B.MB.

Detaining Floryse, I immediately composed a crisp but thorough response, detailing my position.

I shall see you here, now.
F. B. MB. FRASE(G)

I recognised a paradoxical weakness of my strength. As judge, I wished to pass the ultimate sentence. She, as guilty party, did not wish to come hear my words. I felt like a chef who, having assembled all subsidiary ingredients for a Poule Surprise, was on his hand and knees clucking to coax the cooperation of a suspicious chicken.

Gone to the dressmaker.
A. B. MB, along with A.P. and F. ff-M (Duchess)

'Has the master any reply?' asked Florynse with a facetious pretence of cooperation.
When I entered the dining-room for lunch I found the table set for one.
'The mistress?' I asked Florynse. Yes, mistress, indeed.
'Dines out,' said the child.

It being a Friday, I had taken a bath this morning. I like it hot and deep. I dunk myself thoroughly.
I was about to lower myself gingerly into the tub when I saw through the steam a familiar face. A man was submerged to his chin, a foot resting on the tap, and the folds of his belly breaking the surface of suds. He gave me an arrogant stare.
'Ontogeny recapitulates phylogeny,' observed the bather, so revealing himself a scholar. For he had just invoked the profound but obscure tenet of biology that, in its development, the individual passes through some stages of its ancestry.

He had been selfish enough to claim the comfortable place in the bath, at the opposite end to the tap.

'Nematode worms are hermaphrodite,' he declared, 'when they wish to breed, they please themselves.' He then proceeded to soap his arms and shoulders. I noticed he was using my personal sponge.

I'm unused to bathing in public. Save for once—in an informal brothel in Brussels—I haven't shared a bath with any soul since school. Washing is an intimate matter. I prefer to do it alone. I told him so.

'I do, too,' he said.

He was a squat, short, balding man with a wrinkled sun-weathered face; and had but one foot. I was startled to recognise him as myself.

Occasionally in the past—when I have enjoyed some wines—I have had the sensation of rising out of my body to watch myself. But this had always been from just behind and slightly above, as though peering down on my shoulders and the rear of my head. Today was the first instance I'd met myself face to face, and on quite level terms.

'You are me?' I asked. It was a fatuous observation but the most intelligent persons can make fools of themselves when they spare insufficient time for thought.

'You are the mind. I am the body. You cause me much grievance,' he said tetchily, 'with your eccentric whims and ways.'

And it was quite as he said. For looking downwards, I found I was not there. There was no body beneath me. I was disembodied thought and sense, suspended above the floor; and insecure to find that the supports of abdomen and legs had quite absented themselves.

He appeared unperturbed, whistling, smiling smugly, as he lathered himself.

'Together, we are a Cartesian dualism, you and I, a psychosomatic perplex.' He returned his attention to me and spoke a reproof. 'I should sometimes prefer to be left alone. I'd manage very well as a monism.'

'Can you scratch my chin?' I asked, partly out of curiosity but also to relieve the itch. He did so, finding the exact spot without direction, achieving a pleasant relief.

'Now wash your ears,' I said, warming to the game.

'Orders... orders,' he grumbled, yet immediately complied.

'Do you enjoy the water?'

'It is my element. It warms between my toes, trickles down my back, invades between my legs. It buoys me. I like it. It licks and laps my belly.'

'You are happy, then?' I asked, wistfully, for I was not.

'Well...' he was shyly hesitant. 'I have a recurrence of our little problem. A smear of Biedermaa's Unction would ease discomfort.'

'Otherwise?'

'You push too much drink down my gullet. It makes me bleary and lethargic in the morning... and there is the matter of food. I sit down to eat, I savour the smell. I salivate a welcome to the pudding. Then you promptly change your mind and deny me my just dessert.'

'You have other complaints?' Frankly, he had begun to annoy with his endless list of grievances.

'I should like more erotic exercise,' he continued his whining monotone. 'The male organ is like a pressure-hose. It requires regular release.'

'Well, there are domestic difficulties.'

'A fine mess,' he observed, 'I do not wish to be involved or embroiled.'

I had hoped for more cooperation. For we were in this fix together. 'It is my wife's fault. All blames attach to her.' He frowned, hunched his shoulders and shivered. 'The water is getting cold and a body needs some breakfast.' And raising himself up, wobbly on his single foot, he hopped forward, engulfing me, trapping me in his flabby grey flesh, suffusing my consciousness with a range of vulgar notions.

95

I decided that I should, at supper, inform her of her fate. It was surprising to find her in such ebullient spirits. I shot her some firm glances—trying by turn contempt, disdain, irritation and fierce anger. (Druisberg's *Atlas of Physiognomic Expression* shows each of these (pp. 17–256) and details the muscular movements required to achieve their strongest forms.)

Yet she was so insensitive to the moods of her husband as to remain contented and oblivious.

'You will wish to know the cause of my anger. To understand why I took a hammer to your piano stool.'

But she sustained her dumb, insolent disregard.

'Very well, then, I shall fully inform you. . . .'

The woman continued forking red cabbage to her mouth, rapt in shameless congress with her vegetable.

'It is this. . . .'

'Florynse,' the woman called, slovenly, still masticating, her mouth half crammed with cabbage sludge, 'bring some water please, dear girl.'

I could not speak in the maid's presence, as Alyse well knew. Either she has not recognised the gravity of her position. Else she thinks she can oppose me.

It is no wonder I'm bemused. For I am too much and far too many. Friedryk Baa MindeBerg is not alone. We are not alone. We have ourselves. That much is clear, the rest is confused. I hold too many of them within my skin. They fight each other and for escape. A man knows as much by taking his bath.

And the silvered surfaces show me the way. A man can learn much by watching his reflections. When I look in the mirror I do not see myself. Instead there is the face I wear to watch myself. The impertinent fellow has guessed the game. Then realising as much, his expression changes. 'Aha,' he thinks, 'this is not me as the world sees me, but me as I present myself to me.'

Consider the eye.

There! That's the problem.   It does not—nay, cannot—see itself. There must be a second eye. And if there is, does that one see itself?

Proceeding so far, it must be clear that (the observer not observing itself) what is known is always less than what is. Ultimately, this proves god.

Or a mirror. It reflects that which falls before it. The reflection does not reflect upon itself.

A man's mind (I see clearly) is a sequence of mirrors, reflecting reflections. I am a well-endowed man, having at least five mirrors. Alyse, I suspect (from the limits to her comprehension of me and others' matters) has but three. And one of these is plainly cracked.

The mind does not always deploy all its mirrors at once. When I wake in the morning (alone (for my wife does not sleep with me (complaining of my foot (which is a guise (for a pretext (she being a lascivious strumpet)))))) I constitute but one reflective surface. It registers the world—the light through the curtains, playing upon the wall—but not itself. I know the texture of my sheets but have yet to realise who I am and why I sleep alone. Yet then a second mirror is aligned upon the other. 'Quite,' I say, 'it is I'. Then a third... that the I then sees the eye watch the world. Exactly so.

And so it happens that mirrors reflect mirrors upon mirrors. Mind examines the examinations of its analyses. Even before it is breakfast. And depending on the number of mirrors in operation, I am a different man. An unreflective version of me finds the water hot; another Friedryk, bending light through four surfaces, poses his critique of Platonism.

There are, then, (and I tell this only to those versions of me that can understand, for some of me are stupid louts, forever whining about food) a hierarchy of Friedryk Baa MindeBergs. I think we all know the one I refer to. He is dim and grunts a lot. We would all be better off without him. We should never let him out alone, but our minds often weary.

Imagine us all, then, like a file of soldiers. They stand in a line, each seeing those in front. But oblivious of those behind. The frontmost one (whom I have mentioned already) thinks himself alone. He tries to do it all himself. This does not help the rest of us—for he is dolt and dotard, and quite self-seeking to boot.

And the secret of existence (a fearful perplex) is that the soldiers take their turns to fight in the combat that is life. Each goes out with his own self-satisfied view of things, leaving a mess for the next to sort out. And so we pass our days together. No wonder we're in disarray.

Consider Friday—or dreaming even, which is the better example. One reflective surface plays on to another. It pesters and pains. There are some obnoxious images of amputation and talking bones. The dreamer, not knowing what he was doing, terrifies the thinker—who is forced to wake up and take over, quite perplexed, while the body drips cold sweat. 'Only a dream' says the reflective one, turns over and bids the body back to sleep. The unselfconscious dreamer takes over again. Clearly, he's not to be trusted. For within half an hour it happens again. The thinker gets woken up in alarm to sort it all out, all over again.

Or take my wife Alyse. Only one of us wants to be held hot and moist between her silken thighs (yes, indeed; he in the bath). The rest of us have different concerns and do not give a jot, except to grieve over her depravity. Otherwise, we should be far happier discoursing on mammals with our friends or researching pharmaceuticals.

And now I am quite debilitated from the labours of rotating and aligning the mirrors of my mind. And I know that when I lay down my head and close my eyes, those within, who cannot be trusted, will take over my person and shame the spirit of an Academician of Erudition.

Brodskii's Condiment

It is quite inconceivable and yet it has happened. I am not a man to suffer delusions, yet no sooner had I settled myself at my desk than I heard that braying laughter of the deceiving immoralist down below, sounding off like a donkey at his oats.

So she is entertaining he. After all I have said.

I crept to the head of the stairs and saw in the hall his black woollen overcoat hanging brazenly from the hat-stand, confirming my every suspicion.

I thought it time to take action. Words have clearly failed us, and I have been patient and passive too long.

The merits of lamp-oil first commended themselves. But I decided upon Brodskii's Condiment. It is equally combustible but lacks a tell-tale smell. I was most circumspect, quick and quiet. Pouring at least three hundred and fifty millilitres over the shoulders and down the back of the coat, I then introduced a naked flame to the hem. I had forgotten the thrill of fire. The effect was immediate and compelling. I paused long enough to watch the libertine's clothing leap alive with yellow flames, crackling softly.

This should stop their game. I believe that the theory of spontaneous combustion is widely discredited, even amongst laymen. They must surely catch my drift. I am not a man to be trifled with. I give them due warning. It is fortunate for them that I am in a contemplative and philosophical frame of mind. There is a less temperate or reflective portion of my person who is violent and vicious.

He would not have been satisfied in attaching an abstract and indirect message to their clothes.

Wherein lies the individuality of a man? And how may it be scientifically and accurately charted? For we are each fashioned by nature to a precious particularity. Each of us is unique.

The scientists of many nations attend this problem and compete for its resolution. I have recently joined their ranks. A great prize of fame attaches to the solution. Many agencies of state—hospitals, armies, police—should benefit hugely from a capacity to identify men, type and distinguish them.

Lombroso argued for the face; that we each disclose our character through our facade of features. Galton in England claims our distinctiveness lies at the tips of our hands, in the print of our fingers. Each of these attempts holds some particle of truth. The solution, I am convinced, lies in the ears—and that future generations shall take prints of the lobes to establish identity.

There were some startled squeals from below.

Florynse interrupted me with breathless news of a fire. She gave a garbled account. A visitor's coat was in ashes, a hat-stand was beyond salvation, a patch of wallpaper was licked by flame. Some floorboards were lightly charred.

'Was Mr Aaskvist still wearing the garment? Or was he by then undressed?' The child stood panting with a look of pained perplexity.

'I suspect he left a lit pipe in his pocket,' I continued, 'an inadequate intellect might be so dangerously forgetful. Pray tell him I am exceeding angry with him for so threatening my home.'

'But it was not Mr Aaskvist,' said Florynse, looking impatient and bemused. 'It was pastor Briegman's coat.'

'Ah.' This silenced me briefly, but I am quick to analyse new data. 'These things happen to religious persons.' I improvise quickly. 'There was that well-known incident of the burning bush.' All depends on one's face and tone. A man might get away with murder if he properly disciplines

100

his features to display innocent surprise.

'Will the master come?'

'I cannot attend every domestic mishap.' I thought this conveyed a good counterfeit of detached annoyance. 'And instruct your mistress to take more care.'

Why should a mature and sensible woman wish to entertain a pastor on a weekday afternoon? And why should that clergyman laugh?

And I was then seared by a quite upsetting insight. Does my depraved dis-wife entertain a sequence of admirers? Do they queue at the door to fondle her thighs? The logic was obvious. If a wife is degenerate, why suppose her faithful in her infidelity? This answers the enigma of the window. Alyse persists in leaving the living-room window open some few centimetres. She claims it is to disperse my cigar smoke. I suspect it is to allow discreet passage to her paramours.

I recollected the amused glances the pastor had cast me. He would smile without any due cause, as though enjoying some personal joke at my expense.

At the lowest part of a man's pinna there is a fleshy bulge. One reasonably supposes that an excessively large lobe discloses wanton sensuality. Both Alyse and Mr Aaskvist have such unsightly extensions. I gained a print of his ear at the commencement of our acquaintance (he complained, I recall, that the stain would not wash off). I have never asked the pastor for access to his ears. Indeed, I have never sought his conversation or his presence in my home. But I know his aural endowments and how, even in the pulpit, he would finger and pull his lewd bulge as though shamelessly inciting his female congregation, even while they prayed. Yea. By their ears ye shall know them.

I thought back to name and number the harvest of Alyse's male visitors. Her youngest brother Hermaan comes more often than decent family sentiment might dictate. Is there some furtive debauchery between sister and brother. Such things happen, I hear. There was a case reported in the

Bernfor *Gazette* of the affinity between a butcher and his married sister. There was more to the matter than meat.

I once arrived home to find Hoosins in the parlour sneaking conversation with my wife. I remembered then wondering what could be the subject of such rapt debate—given that his interests are so similar to my own. He pretended to have called to see me. Yet when we came to talk ourselves there were long pauses with little to fill them.

There might be many such—Dobyn the persistent cloth merchant, that pianist with the cleft plate whose name I can never remember, Berthe's nephew Adolphus who calls on Saturday, Mauriz the gardener, Alburt the marine artist. She talks to them all. I have seen her. She catches them alone.

If she nets a pastor, who might she then exclude? Perhaps she entertains the town. The guide books might recommend her as one feature of our national hospitality. I shall not talk to her till I get the proper measure of her corruption. Yet I shall defend myself.

I walked out to purchase the neccessary sanitary prerequisites. The merchant extorted an extra fourteen ffenyngs to deliver them to the topmost floor of the house.

It so many years since I have done such work. But principle is simple and the practice facile. It is just a matter of binding together the small units of construction with slow-drying adherent, into the required shape. I mixed the mortar in the basin in my room. Soon I had worked up a fine sweat and was breathing heavily from the effort. But it was good to engage in manual labour and tax that animal within me. If I make him work for his supper, he may be too tired for lewd pursuits.

'But what are you doing Friedryk?' Alyse was clearly too dismayed to sustain her cold reserve. The garrulous maid must have told her of the unusual deliveries.

It was nonetheless not difficult to discern my activity. A

102

child of five would have recognised my purpose easily enough; a gibbon or chimpanzee would have grasped the idea; a distracted goose might have got an inkling. It is a feature of our time, and the misapplicaton of education, that all find complexity and sophistication in the house of simplicity.

'I am effecting a slight domestic improvement,' I said tersely but did not turn to face the woman.

'A wall. . . . You are building a wall?' she asked, as though we are playing charades or some guessing game in the parlour.

'Indeed.' And when I had finished that I should build one more.

'Why, Friedryk?' she spoke a tired sadness.

'I seek more privacy.' The first wall was to brick up the arch that connected our bed-chambers. It seemed a mocking irony for the orifice to remain. Then I should have a section erection in the passage-way to seal the other entry. I desired no such opening. Better a brick frame to a firm door. There will be three strong locks and one set of keys.

Artisans who perform this repetitive task each day might have achieved a cleaner finish. But my wall was robust and firm enough. She'd need a hammer and chisel, then a monumental passion, to hack her way through.

'Are you ill, Friedryk?'

Now why should a man hearty in labour, and evidently enjoying the venture, strike his wife as sick?

Her question was yet another symptom of the lack of understanding intercourse between us. It occurs to me that there were never two persons more ill-suited—by intelligence, interest, height or temperament—to the mission of marriage. I think I tried hard enough to slow my mind to consider the anatomy of blouses, natural history of bootees, physiognomy of corsets. But she never tried to ascend to my perch. She abuses my monkeys and shuns all amphibians. When I moved my scrutiny from toads to marsupials, she showed no enthusiasm. Though my mind tracked their infinite variety, they were all the same to her.

'You exhaust yourself, husband. Stop... rest. Take a drink.'

For she lacks all depth or insight into the problems of others. There is ever some simple solution of stupefying banality. For melancholy, she prescribes herself a bonnet with white felt orchids. Whenever I am flummoxed by some paradox of science, she advises the metal stimulus of warm milk. On the death of Florynse's father she bought the girl a crucifix. To repair the loss? Or perhaps they prayed together for the magic of a resurrection.

'A brandy, Friedryk, to soothe you?'

And now, because I loathe her in her depravity, she thinks me ill and proposes the remedy of alcohol. It requires more than the distillate of wine to repair our sorry disunion.

'There,' I said, for the first wall was all but completed. 'Now our rooms are quite separate. There is no connecting door. I shall not cross your bed again.'

'You are unwell, Friedryk.' And she tried to clutch me by the arm. And she had proceeded from tentative enquiry to confident diagnosis. She knew I was unwell. And on what evidence? Because I did not wish to lie on her warm belly, stroke her flanks, touch the soft firmness of her chest, be clutched in her fierce thighs, sniff her hair, lick the labyrinth of her ear?

Yet as she turned from me, sniffling and reproachful as a scolded child, it was as if my fire was doused, the frost bit to my marrow. I felt hollow and shrunk. There is no companion. How may a man subdue his solitude?

And this is her crime. That she promises warmth and care, refuge for my sorrows and body. And at root it is deceit, flimsy and transparent. For she is a betraying strumpet. So I have sealed my path to her bed, and made concrete my resolution. I had a dog once when I was a boy. I shall have a dog again—a puppy new to the world. It will sleep upon my eiderdown and snuggle into my curves. It will be naughty—for so puppies are—but I shall train it and teach it to walk to heel. When I am too severe, it will lick my face and hands. Perhaps, I might train it to retrieve my foot.

My first dog, Sammi, a black and white snipehund with large brown eyes, drowned in an experiment on anaerobic respiration, being unable to adapt to changed conditions. Now I shall have another and take the better care of it, and pose more reasonable demands. I favour a bitch. They are more faithful than a dog. This is well known.

Nonetheless, I shall take a little brandy—if only to calm my mind and settle my stomach.

I have been worse used—long ago in North Aafryka. Though not a superstitious man, the events left me with my one enduring foible. I cannot bear for my boot laces to be tied tight. Constrictions to my feet raise me to the pitch of panic. My forehead weeps sweat. I heave and pant.

A man has but two feet. When one is spent, he must take full care of the other.

Alone on the Essuerra Plains, I search out the ruins of Marek. Rising from excited scrutiny of a carved stone, I find myself surrounded by Effirs. They are nomadic thieves: now they have chanced upon me. I am much apprehensive and dismayed. They are not pleasant men. They trade in slaves and are known to bear scant regard for the dignity and lives of men. It is documented that they break the right leg of any servant—saving themselves the expense of manacles, the task of tethering, or the labour of recapturing absconders. They think to ensure the discretion of those in their employ by pulling out tongues and piercing ear-drums. Those unfortunate enough to be selected to attend the Effir women are emasculated by crudely violent surgery—which it is unlucky to survive.

Their religion pronounces these practices virtuous, denounces strangers as undomesticated beasts, and yet deifies a poisonous beetle. Despite having no monuments, writing, science or music, they think themselves very fine. Their art they work in other's flesh.

Five of these persons gather languidly about me, watching impassively. They wear long robes of pink or white, like so many babes, dressed for their cots. They give a deceptive impression.

'No man would buy him. He is old and a dwarf,' one of them remarks.

'He carries a bag of possessions. He is a rat with a cache.'

'He could tend goats,' said another, and seizing my arms behind me he forces the horn handle knife between my lips. They chatter excitedly as they examine my teeth.

'The teeth lie. He is older than they say.' They speak a corrupt tongue but I know its source. I decide it time to reveal that I understand them well enough and can speak more grammatically than they. It is important to assert my significance lest they consider me subordinate.

'Which of you is chief?' I demand to be told. They are surprised at my remark and huddle together, hissing hurriedly through tight lips.

'I am a chief in my own nation,' I warn them, 'and must not be ill-used. My king is very powerful.' Yet none replies to me.

'I come to bring you a gift.' I look to my belongings for a satisfactory sacrifice. 'Here is a trowel and a water-bottle.'

'A sparrow can shit,' observes one sagely, 'but no man thanks it.'

'There is also my time-piece and a leather belt with a brass buckle. I give you these to pay for safe-conduct.'

'We do not ask a camel to fart. The sound is as bad as the smell.'

'The fig need not agree with the teeth,' says another.

'I wish to give you my knife and compass,' I continue. 'To pay respect to your noble peoples.' They are a proud tribe. I try to win them by flattery.

'A fleeced goat grows new hair, but a goat stew makes no new gravy.

And binding my hands behind my back they throw me

106

rudely to the ground. They open my bag and studiously examine the contents, patiently discussing each item.

'This tells the night it must grow dark.' He throws my watch aside.

'It directs the sun where to rise and set.' The compass does not excite them either.

They spread out the map and examine it soberly. 'In case he forgets, this tells him what is sand and which is sea. When he meets a river he can call to it by its proper name.'

'There are no valuables?' One for them shakes the empty bag with disgust.

'I shall have the hoofings,' says one, as though, having examined a rotten apple, he had found one edible portion. And placing his feet in my groin, tugs at one boot with a ferocious jerk. He seems unfamiliar with laces; these being another deficit of their culture. I fear he may pull apart my legs whilst quite crushing my nethers. Yet the boot finally parts my foot, yielding to his enthusiasm.

'Wait,' I say, my face wrinkled by grimace and watered by tears. 'There is a simpler way.'

This is my mistake.

'The sheep instructs the shearer,' says the savage, smiling briefly. Clearly he misunderstands my suggestion. We each think to our own culture: I to the convenience of laces, he to the incisiveness of the blade. For he rises and, with a full swing of his sword, lops my leg at the ankle. He clutches up the foot its container of boot, and begins to excavate with his knife, carving out shards of my foot to fall by his.

There was no pain, but a violent throbbing—the hurt came later. I thrust the stump deep into the sand to quench the flow of life from me.

'Falcons soar, camels walk, but worms and beggars must crawl,' said the one with my boots. Then they turned and were gone, over the mound of a dune, leaving a trail of me behind them.

But there are softer organs than a foot, and some that

lace a duplicate. And she has seared my heart with her cautery iron. And who might come to find and nurse me this time?

It occurs to me that of the manifold conveniences and luxuries our civilisation has spawned, I have at least one of each except of friend.

Caffeine

There is no puppy to be had. No snipehund. There was. There shall be. Now is not the time. Mr Siibelyus's bitch has just pupped. But they are too young to be parted of their mother. They squeak and burrow, blind at her paps. And there is no other litter in the town. None. That I know of.

Instead, I have procured a Striped Salamander. He is a decent enough amphibian. But he is not companionable. It is a long, and thankless, task to try convert a salamander to friend. They are slow to learn, lethargic and—being poikilothermic—not the most emotional of beasts. He lies languid in the shallows of his tank. Often he gulps; sometimes he twitches his foot. An hour ago he slowly swept his tail through an arc of thirty degrees. But this is not enough to coax the sustained scrutiny of an intelligent man. He does not turn to look when I talk to him. Like Alyse, he responds to my touch with distaste. He gives little reward or warmth. I do not intend to slight him. He does his best and observes his instincts. Yet it is hard to count him as friend.

Benjamyn, my monkey, is withdrawn and cold. He could give more. But he teases me, pretending indifference. I try to coax him with some games—hop, step and jump, hand ball, hunt the grape—but he does not join with me.

He is opaque. Benjamyn is withdrawn. I suspect Mr Darwin undervalues him. A monkey is more than we suppose. Take music. I bought him a drum. He yawns and pretends disdain. Yet when I am but a little time gone, he commences to play, beating his intricate rhythms. I hear distantly and scurry back to see the performance. An artist, who will not suffer interruption, he promptly stops. Undaunted, I encourage him. To offer him more scope, I purchase for him a more demanding instrument. A xylophone. He teases again, for he has a dark sardonic temperament. It is not his way to encourage a man. He plays the fool to satirise my expectations—pushing the hammers in to his nose, banging his drum with them, or else reclining upon the instrument. But he does not fool me. I exit the animal house and bang hard the door behind me. I walk away, sound loud my steps on the stone floor. Then I stop, remove my shoes and tip-toe back in stockinged feet. Listen at the door. He persists in his animal capers for some minutes. Assured he is alone, a hush falls. It is broken by him sounding his scale—B flat, for he is a melancholy ape. Then he begins. *Allegro moderato*. Ravishingly contemplative. It is the first movement of Schubert's last pianoforte sonata which Benjamyn has transposed for xylophone. How he plays his pauses! A man's heart is shaded by lyrical sadness. What *legato*, and what fastidious *tempi*. Schubert prepares to die. Benjamyn speaks his soul.

A spirit that can scale such heights of empathy might pause to comfort a friend.

'Sometimes a man feels hollowed, Benjamyn. . . . It is as if all that once lived in him is frozen and shrunk. He rattles empty in his solitude.'

But the ape that plays rapturously the *Andante Sostenuto*, gives not a glance to his master. Instead, he chews his blanket.

'A little consolation, Benjamyn. Some small show of concern. . . . If only to repay the debt of three years' fruit and care.'

He shuffles guiltily some moments. Then he turns his back.

'I might buy you a pianoforte. Or you could play the mistress's. She is leaving our residence soon.'

But he snorts and curls himself up. He prefers solitude to

healthy society. I see clearly he wants nothing more than for me to leave.

A man must tread his lonely furrow. If none is there to light his way, he must illumine the path for himself.

Today, I commence the C's. I make fast progress. Alone. We think it harmless enough. Our coffee and our tea. I have concentrated some caffeine. Berthe was uncooperative . She thinks excessive my order of four pots of coffee.

'Does the master entertain an orchestra? Have they fallen asleep in his study?'

I pay the bills. The coffee beans are from my purse. I rent her time. There is no call for complaint. Despite my generosity of an explanation, she fails to comprehend the principles of distillation.

It was exceedingly bitter (8), the treacly tar residue of ten litres of good strong coffee. It takes a man with a rush, hitting him like a hammer. At first, he thinks his whole body will be crushed by the sudden weight. Of his mind. His veins spurt. He feels the shooting rush of his fluids. His body is a system of connecting ducts, holding fierce hydraulic forces. It is a wonder he does not burst. So high is he pressured. It seems as though he is lifting from the floor.

The mind races. All is clear. He sees. He knows. He understands.

Words are too poor. They cannot keep pace with mind. They are sluggard stragglers. Thought has passed their slouching forms and disappears from their sight. Even when you wait for them to crawl up, they are breathless and can bear no weight. They are silhouettes. I need some side of them, colour and sharp edge. They must prance and dance, jump and twist, if they hope to keep pace with thought.

And how am I meant to work with them—for my science? That noun, she consorts with fish-traders and cow-herds. I smell the taint when I reach for that verb. I put it back. I know where it has been. Widow Bergmeir has used it for usury. Her grandson has picked his nose with it. Fornicators have shared their crumpled, stained sheets with that epiphet. It has been in the pig-sty trawled through slurry. The pastor dropped that phrase from his pulpit. I shall not stoop to gather his discards and debris. How may I use these words when I find them so defiled, tarnished, insanitary and ill-used? I shall not suck up the spittings of another man's mouth.

if A^* $>$= words $/a-z/$ 1–n (0–10), then all is corruption and filth. And what hope ($>$0) remains.?

I see clearly (10). All is obvious. Some (1) are clean enough—poikilothermic, bivalvular, hominoid, crepuscular, galactopoiesis, kermesite, lachrymation, preganglionic, hepatocellular. There's a whiff of cigar smoke hanging on them, for they waft from the lounge of the Academy. No matter, I am prepared to share with colleagues. At least a man knows that peasants have not sucked them and spat them through their brown and broken teeth. And no women have nibbled at them in the salon.

Prophylactic, that's clean enough, and urethroscope, sinciput, psoriasis and prurigo. The doctors have washed off the mucus and phlegm and doused them down with carbolic.

But fish, flesh, hole, smell—and, and—induce in me spasms of vomiturition.

Best say little and keep clean. For as soon as you speak, you share words, from mouth to mouth, gobbing back and forth, dribbling. And though you are clean, what of you partner? Perhaps they are promiscuous conversationalists—infecting you with spit from the market, fluids from the throats of infected transients. I have tried the prophylaxis of monogamy. But where has this got me? The strumpet talks to every man and leaks their juices over me.

This is a most uncivil war. They sound off in mind, screaming their competing claims, howling, whining, hectoring. There is more sound that a head can bear. All squabbling and rancour.

I am not afraid to name them and honestly state their characters.

There is the frothing lout. He is an idle, uncouth fellow who wishes no more than to sleep away the day, unless there is a whiff of petticoat or he is stirred from his dribbling reverie by the music of the dinner gong. He accosts Florynse and makes shaming proposals (the child wisely declines). It pains me to harbour him. I am forever called out to apologise for his conduct and clean up the mess he leaves behind him. I know him as Friedii, though he claims my full name and brags himself Count and Academician. But it is sheer cant. He knows nothing of biology, save the howl of his own appetites. And when he wants, he demands to have his satisfactions gross and immediate. When he does not have his way, he is savage, screams and raves. Then he tries to seize the controls and purloins the power of my hands.

This morning he was most violent. We had our first fracas early. I was thinking of the exoskeleton of arthropods whilst dressing, being prompted by the curves of an empty boot. So engrossed was my mind, I cast no sidelong glances to monitor the clothing of my flesh. I woke from contemplation to find my feet brazen in yellow socks! These were bought for me by Alyse to celebrate my name-day. Naturally, I had hidden the vulgar items away at the back of my drawer.

It was he. He had snatched them from concealment and thrown them upon my feet. He is insatiable and ravening when he sees gaudy colours. And irascible when I seek to thwart him. We struggled for control of our hands. No sooner had I removed one sock than he'd replaced the other. I twisted his hand, he sunk his nails into my wrist. It took some time to subdue him. I told him clearly that if he would pay the merchants' bills, I should let him select the

113

socks. He turned sulky and silent. Either he'd taken my point or was dribbling thoughts of flesh.

When I had dressed (replacing those stockings with my habitual grey) I walked off to my study and passed Florynse on the route. I nodded to her soberly as is my wont. There can be too much sentiment and familiarity between master and maid. I prefer the business brisk and formal. And the lewd rascal, quite undermining my intentions, scratching the polished patina of our practice, snatched the use of my hand and laid it on the girl. He flung the fingers on the warm, firm swell of her left buttock. I was insufficiently fast in wresting control of the hand to prevent him stroking, then making a digital insinuation.

Of course we both blushed crimson, the girl and I, whilst the rascal laughed lasciviously.

'Beast,' I hissed at him.

'Prude,' he chortled.

'Take no heed, Florynse. It was not I,' I reassured the child. 'It was him.' But the girl retreats backward from me in silence, her hands protectively about her chest, with a scowl of recrimination. It is not her fault. She is not to know the difference 'twixt him and me. We're all the one to her.

'Pig,' I told him and boxed his ear (which is the left). 'Rest assured, Florynse. He shall be punished. Why, for that he'll forfeit his lunchtime pudding.'

And how is a man to maintain or enhance his dignity if there is one within him who proposes to go through life lubriciously, debauching servants in his yellow socks?

Yet if I am to do good work, I must concentrate. But when I focus my mind to close scrutiny he wanders lewdly away with my limbs.

And then there is the Count. An urbane man and social. It's hard to fault his manners for he substitutes propriety for thought. Take him out for dinner and he's perfectly presentable, hovering close to the elbow of charm. He might go so far as to commit a joke. Ask him of the Vronsky

114

Settlement and he'll say something quite immemorable, for he's master of the inconsequential aside, tyro of the trivial, maestro of piffle and piddle. Whatever the topic, he'll find a perfectly unremarkable remark, to offend neither republican nor royalist. Munitions manufacturer and pacifist can forget him with equal ease. Neither angler nor worm might take the slightest offence, for he's careful to show no side. He will toss his small pebble into the pond of conversation, it will sink to its proper resting-place, and without perturbing the ducks. But tax him on Science and you'll soon see the lack. He's happy enough shooting cormorant or burrowing for badger, but when it comes to distinguishing electrophoresis and photoelectrolysis he cannot pass the test. Worse, he doesn't care. Not a damn.

Ask him to imagine. He will consult his book of etiquette and advise you, with a wry smile and no semblance of offence, that protocol deems it impolite.

He's pleasant enough. But there's something significant lacking. Despite his solidity, you cannot help but think him vacuous.

He it was that married Alyse and welded me into this fix. My mind was then committed to serious work. I thought it safe to depute him to the task of winning a suitable spouse, so leaving me free to think. He seemed well suited to the long journeys, aimless conversations, speculative dinners involved in searching out a good woman of sound family. Here lay my flaw. He selected someone to suit his anodyne taste. And she was so undiscriminating as to find him pleasant. So imagine her surprise when she first met me. These things happen. And who can wonder that a deaf matchmaker should select a dumb bride.

It is not just Alyse that prefers him. 'But where is that not unnice man?' They think. 'He is so fluent, and so interesting about whatever it was, I forget. He said nothing to offend, and all without pausing for thought. He drank barely any wine and left prompt and polite at eleven. Such a shame about his foot. But so pleasant to find a man who does not overstay or overestimate his welcome. We must remember his name and ask him again. He might entertain deaf Aunt Maathilde and help arthritic Doriis cut her meat.'

It is frankly shaming to keep his company; mortifying that persons should prefer his presence to my own. For he is a ninny and half-baked noodle, forever prattling about the weather and democracy (when, in truth, he has not the slightest intention to involve himself with either). But the booby pipes up his piece.

'I think we are due some rain,' he says. Really! Those were indeed his words. As if his confidantes, the elements and atmosphere, had just whispered as much in the Club. As though rain were some moral payment from the heavens, which were overdrawn on their account to us. As if a man cares. As if he might challenge or oppose if he did. As if we had no more pressing calls on our time than to discuss the deposition of small gobbets of water.

It is all quite humiliating to be mistaken for him. Yet he is more in demand than I. I know they prefer I should trot him out to bray his bit. When he speaks of the stiffness of shirt collars, the unpunctuality of trains or our civic duties, they smile their interest. But should I interrupt him to relay news of the progress of knowledge—of advances in renal physiology, the mental stimulus of alkaloid, a new typology of toads—why then they are silent, smirk or gaze to their feet, then bid me a brisk 'good-day'.

So I am bound up within the very same skin as a lecher and a booby, forced to listen to the howls of the one and the prattles of the other.

'Let us say something inconsequential to Duckstaatd. Perhaps, we might mention the rising price of monographs. Or would that sound provocative?'

'No. I wish to insert myself in a woman. That one there will do.'

'Silence.' I bid them both. 'Man was made for more.'

'But we could smile at Hoosins and ask of his health.'

'Then fuck his wife,' shrieks the other. 'And, after, hump

116

his daughters.'

And how I wish that I could shed them, the tawdry businesses of the flesh and inanities of the dinner table, and be truly alone in my head.

And I? The real I? But a humble servant of science, prophet of the verities. Zealot and missionary of fact. Explorer, hacking at the undergrowth of dogma, slashing aside the thick stems of ignorance, slicing through the tangled brambles of superstition, with the sharp machete of my mind. For through this jungle lies a clearing of truth, where all may bathe in the radiance of fact. A man must fight through the dank gloom to clear the path for those behind. A man must follow this route. Else he is nothing but excretory tubing, pumped by his lusts. Mouthing platitudes to excuse himself.

Cannabis sativa

I smoke my pipe. I defend the high ground where they cannot catch me unawares.

They have me surrounded. The only path out lies through the centre of their territories down from this peak through the high-walled labyrinthine paths into which their caves are hewn. It is their land and they know its slightest crannies and recesses, turns and twists, escarpments, flats and terraced slopes. No man might hope to survive the ambush. Having once ventured out, a man so incautious would find they had blocked his advance and covered his retreat. There would remain no alternative but to stand and fight outnumbered.

No. I shall remain within the defensive walls of my stockade. I think they hope to starve me out. They know I have but few supplies. In truth, I have small quantities of brandy, bread, cannabis, cocaine, cantharides, chloroform, chloral hydrate.

So begins the trial of my hunger and their patience. Perhaps I am lost and there is naught I can do to sustain my defence. For they will wear me down, fray my nerves with mock attacks, force me to the strain of unrelenting vigilance, all the while starving me out. Yet a man has to defend what is true and good. So I commence my fight with the aboriginals. We each have our superiority; theirs of number, mine of right.

There is also that force that all explorers hold over rude and superstitious natives. The strength of science and system, which the savage lacks. She has her cunning and her wiles, the audacities of ignorance, the frenzies of her lusts, the simple confidence of a soul attuned to nature. But I carry within me physics and mechanics, writing, geography and logic. With a little a man might contrive a lot. Some string and wood, with fabric for the sling, could be fashioned to light artillery—soundly advised by the rudiments of engineering. Desperation feeds ingenuity. Much might be made of the blanket, belt, mirror, ink and tin-tacks through an intricate application of method.

I also have about me some artefacts of the modern world. I might fashion some trinkets and try to negotiate a trade. Some savages go to dizzy ecstasy when they sight a tin can, pocket knife or copper chain. They might be so greedy or excited as to give time by trading some sorghum or chicken.

Above all these, I have my gun and two cartridges. I should perfer to effect a bloodless escape. It would pain me to shoot a woman, whatever her tribe and customs. But if I must, I will—and save the second barrel for myself. They shall not have me alive.

There is the sour tang of dead flesh upon the air. Somewhere in this part lies the decaying remains of another traveller, or else some sacrificial victim.

I know of their rites and rituals. A person may tell them from their gaudy dress: they wear ornamental helmets with crude motifs of their totem plants. They are frightful fond of ornaments and sometimes jangle from the metals and beads about their necks and wrists. Some pierce holes in their ears, poking through ornaments on hooks which hang heavy, stretching the lobes. Their bodies they smear with juices and essences, which gives them their singular smells, and enables a man to sniff them out in their hiding places. Much time is spent amongst them eyeing the other's ornament and decorations, sniffing another's odours on which they candidly remark. A perceptive visitor to their realm might suppose this fixation with superficial appearance compensates for their lack of a written culture. When a group of people are loath to write, gossip and chatter are summoned to fill the vacuum.

The torso they clothe tight to so reveal, by concealing, the singular and distinctive curves and swells to their unlikely physique. No civilised man is structured thus. Below their waists, which are accentuated by constricting belts, their skirted clothes bulge wide over violently swollen hips.

Facial adornent is commonplace. They paint their lips, in violent shades of red and orange; smear ochres on their cheeks, paint brows and eyelids with charcoal. Their hair they grow long, often coiling it up upon their scalp and there affixing it with iron prongs.

They talk fast and through a wide range of pitch; squeaking, then guttural; chattering then shrieking. And by their tone, when a traveller knows them well enough, their volatile and turbulent moods may be divined. Though they are prone to deceit—using their voices by turns to leak their passions or feign some effect.

In the posture of a missionary did F enter amongst them, carrying the torch for the standards of civilised men, regarding Her curious features, exposing B's own, divesting of caution, throwing Baaself upon Her hospitality, laying the weight of B's corpus upon them, penetrating Her secret recesses, watching apart when refused an access, alternating twixt congress and silence, learning what F might of the secret chambers of Her nature, progressing from the broad path of acquaintance around the bend to familiarity, pushing further to intimacy, and the dark interior of Her moisture, building piece by part B's understanding of the aboriginal Minde, witness to the volatility of Her passion, simplicity of Her exuberances, deceits, conceits and charming candours, Her aptitudes and limitations, Her ironical or mocking answers to the crawls of logic, Her irritation with theory, partial literacy and stunted numeracy, the constancies and inconsistencies of those principles She used in the stead of morals—briberies, favouritisms, conscriptions—Her webs

120

of friendships and net of animosities, the currencies of Her trade, Her payment systems and exaction of cost, burgeoning, haggling, banter, Her expectorations of gifts, Her hunting and gathering, subsidence economy, the fastidiousness of Her bathing rituals, the fixed preoccupation with facades and surfaces, the complexities of Her toilette, the intricacies of Her b-ody ornaments and adornment, Her art in panting Her Flesh, the obsessional concern with the patterns and shapes She makes of Her hair, and although these insights into Her native culture prospered, and offered the material for more than one fat volume, there grew some dischance between us, built of flimsyarity, reflected in a diminution of Her curiosity for me, and F for them, such that She no longer parading before me to coax B's intention, began, F saw, to conceal some abstractions from B's gaze, and this understandable distancing was associated with a father, but more insidious, effect of them regarding me with some semblance of grievance, albeit ill-defined, that implied, yet never clearly stated, that She believed me to have defaulted on some constrictual terms F had not even suspected, but which might nonetheless have existed in Her primitive minds, for though garrulous of trivia, She presumes too much, staying tacit on matters closer to Her hearts, and so it transpired F felt less welcomed than when F had first ventured into Her land, and became recipient of indifferent or suspicious glances, focus of her ill-rumour, F suspected, and discerned in expressions, to which Her highly mobile and flexible faces are particularly prone, nor was it much longer before this presactiment of ill-ease was confined by more definite and material gestures on Her part, and here F became naturally concerned for it is well documented how fast the savage Minde might shift from grievance to grudge, and thence to hostility, from which it is but a short disdain to open aggression, and some explorers, it has been reported, having contracted some inadvertent broach of the parochial local prettycol have been summarily despatched, by a sharp blow to the cranium, perhaps, delivered by a

121

knobbled or spiked club of eBony, or poisoned, sipping some bitter, foetid brew from a ceremonial chalice, mistaking the lethal cup for obscure compliment, and all these even whilst they feel bathed in the warmth of the natal hospitality, enjoying the primitive fair as best they might, nibbling with a display of gusto, whilst furtively secreting in his pocket the most repugnant items of the unlikely repast, the lower bowel of a warthog, perchance, or pickled gristle of goose-foot, or mealy-bug porridge, and logic must reveal that such occlusions are more frequent than reports of them, for dead men write no journals, publish no scholarly monographs, nor do they report back to the Institutes of Geography of his home nation, nor relay his travails to his organs of public semination, and it would only be if the victim and companions who were not similarly despatched, F propose, would his fate be revealed to civilisation through the agency of a third-parcel, it must then be concluded, as B's own experience have shown, that foreign Parts and persons are yet more dangerous than is first supposed, by virtue of the Bias within accounts towards the reports of survivors who, it must be supposed, are more favourably disposed than would Be those dead, and consequently denied the right to document his demise, further, it must be presumed, that those parts of our globule which are not discoursed in the Geographers' literature are not necessarily unexplained, for the evidence that none have returned does not logically dictate that none have gone, F became justifiably cautious in B's dealings, and, further, cautious of displaying B's caution, (yet resolved, nonetheless to exercise it), for nothing may be so provocative to the native Minde as a sow of suspicion by a stranger amongst them, for b! so reveals himself as disrespectful and distrustful (if She be innocent) or has guessed Her malign intent (if such She have) and, if the latter, She, so discovered, may see no gain in sustaining any lingering pretence of amiability, and would then feel incited as to proceed so far as to part him of a foot, bind him hand and leg, purloin him of beasts and burdens, strip him of clothes, smash his compass, and depart with his boots, or entirely snuff his person, and bearing this in his Minde, whilst carefully concealing it in his face, so as not to precipitate the very catastrophe b! fears, the explorer is posed the perplex, for, as civilised Baa, b! is loath to kill his hosts merely to ensure his own B-ing, on unsubstantiated suspicions, nor himself suffer that fate, yet this consign is now pursed, for the point is reached, and there is no departure from its terms and conditions, which prevailing, can be divined as those of raw hostility, which has, declared this day, found me under siege as She whoop and chortle at the walls of B's defence, rattling the stockade, cajoling and coaxing F should open up to them, and promising safe conduct, or, by turns, threatening Her vengenance should F not, and when F examine B's conduct during ther period of b!'s sojourn amongst them F can honestly find no misconduct on B's part, nor negligence, nor default, nor meant offence, no malice, no harm to deserve or warrant Her threat, and concluding such must suppose Baaself to have touched upon some raw nerve, exposed some flaw within Her temperament, the strata of some noxious fault beneath the crust, which having irritated must bear the consequences of the turbulent angers so ignited, concluding, them, that what transpires is the conflict between the civilised and ordered Minde and the unmasked depths of oval within Her primitive hurts, and in this contest of infamy and order Baa must fight, for the preservation not only of his own and noble person but for the qualities and principles which have nurtured him to civilised and wholesome nature, and it must strike him that b! defends not only the integrity of his kin, through which b! is loath to leak his vital juices, but that wall which is built of bricks which are the institutions of his civilised culture, which b! will not see breached, nor torn assunder, such that b! fights a just war, not merely for himself, but as proxy for science, the piano and pencil, railway and manners, morality and microscope, even in terror in this tropic, b! fights for them, for the in roads that Minde has made over disorder, for the triumph of system over superstition, mediciny against the louse, water-closet over ordure, bridge over water, yet F had considered so little Her primitive forces, the spells She cast, the shadows She make fall on a Minde, the sharp needles She push through his ears with the shrieks of their incantations as She seek to summon shaman powers against him, invoking pestilence and itch, flea and bat, fever and spectre, ghoul and rat, hoodo and hex, and though a Baa not believe the malediction, yet b! is not immune, for the traveller has seen, indeed, the hale and hearty fall and wither like autumn leaf, punished even for allowing his goat to stray on another man's millet field, or spurt blood through his navel for defying the augury of sortilege or myomancer, or turned into caprolite, all by the correct curse, of fument, fugh or foutra, and the herdsman writhing bemaggotted of kidney for slighting the uzzard-priest or neglecting the proper gift of a chicken to his wife's sister's marriage banquet, and thus She invoke against me the jet faucet of malice, invade B's head, make itch and splotch, of nose and nethers, but a Baa must not scratch for making worse the wound, and admitting the power, for to concede Her influence is to invite it in, bathe it with belief, till it bursts within him, and b! cannot fight it, for b! has bid it enter, grow and clutch him in its pustular fingers, so F say F do not itch, nor see the boils, nor blisters, and there are no furnuncles, a Baa has nothing amiss to his skin , it smooth and soft as a baby's wumpitte, and F will not let the voices enter neither, nor allow those images the registration on B's sight, for She may be fought and so dismissed, it requires but fortitude and tight concentration, B-ing assured that science cannot allow them, no mediciny accost them of its list of ills, and the physicist knows them not, for She are immaterial and so cannot tinker with a Baa or molest his molecules, or make him writhe with wriggle, so there is not itch (to B's nostrils of nethers, therefore F shall not scratch, there B-ing no call, and these sights (of faces and masks in uncompanionable grimaces (looming))) are but anomalises, mere elusions, caused only by brief

124

moelcular storms in a man's tea cup, as are the odours (of sulphur and Flesh (reducing to its consitutuents)), and B-ing alone, hear no voices—moans, groans, whimpers, shrieks—which are too indistinct to be understood.

Rested, a Baa feels much improved and soundly-witted throughout the gamut of his faculty box. He is reassured of the fortitudes of his stockage heights and firm walledness. And though She have huffed and puffed, beating at his barriers, She have effected no entrancing. Very well. And b! has repulsed voice barrage and spirit insertion. Sinistrals do not penetrate F. Neither cantrips of rune-mongers B. Evidentially. Quite.

Mind-resistant buffer, molecules, lotions, woman-resistant estrangements, all pockled man-surfacings even. Even. Ullage. Frottage. Punklings diminish with that. The lithe numberlings available to the exercise, precisely chorus so, graph-plotted, method-strictured, report, straight-lined through seven points. It B-ing no coincidence there are seven. For this muscular little cardinal, faithful in long-service of science, reports of parade even from reveille to last-postings.

The number seven guards it safe.

Cocaine

on the third day

I write of the relief of a man's siege, of the transport of his spirits—far stronger than alkaloid of caffeine may effect—when is freed, elevated from the prison of despond to the peak of joyous liberty.

I had thought that they were savages, hacking at my gate. Gaining neither entry nor reply, they called through to me:

'Baa MindeBerg. Let us in.' And theirs was the voice of my own people—low-pitched, authoritative, speaking reason and my name.

'Who is it?'

'It is us,' they confirmed.

'You are men of Europe.'

'We are.'

I thought to give them a test. Having endured these long nights of torment, and holding firm, I should not now succumb to sorcery or apparition.

'Who or what is Jaarlsberg?' I demanded to know of them, 'Man or cheese? Knock once for the former; twice for the latter. Then tap once more if Schubert is dead.'

'Bang ... bang ... tap.'

'And a carbonic solution? It is alkaline or acid?'

'Acid,' shouted one.

'Yet dilute,' said the other.

No savages could know of this. I realised I was saved.

'Are you alone?'

'We are.'

So I pulled back the bolt to the gate, opening enough for them to slide through, quickly sealing the defences behind us.

I had seen strange sights when the European traveller seeks to adjust himself to the Aafrykan climate. I favour light linen and a sturdy boot. But each must find his own compromise between formality and comfort. They wore top hats, scarves, thick woollen overcoats, black suits, and silk cravats over crisp starched shirts of spotless white.

'Baa MindeBerg. I presume,' said the taller of the two, a stout, towering bearded man. He smiled soberly, extending a broad hand to clutch mine in a fierce grasp.

'How did you find me?'

'We heard reports. We were informed. Your family worried for your welfare.'

'Then you are my saviours.' I embraced them in turn.

'From what do we save you?'

'From savages. The local peoples.'

'I'm sure the people of our nation are as good as any other,' said the shorter, gruffly.

'Am I not a savage?' enquired the bearded one facetiously.

'Indeed not. You know science and trousers. You wear beard and tie.'

'Whereas you, yourself, are naked,' he observed.

'It is more comfortable in this clime.'

'Have you been drinking?' the beard asked solicitously.

'Only brandy. There is no water left.It is fortunate you come now. I have only two bottles of spirits remaining . . . and some cocaine to keep me calm.'

'Do you know who we are?' asked the bearded one.

'Explorers? Missionaries?'

'We are doctors.'

'And I too!—Grosse Collegium. '67. Faculty of Natural Sciences.'

'But we are doctors of medicine.'

'There is much to observe in these parts,' I said, 'Fevers,

agues, shakes. epidemics, bilharzia, kwashiorkor.'

'Is that so?' asked the beard. I have noticed of medical men that they resent others knowing anything of their science. They think themselves not unspecial.

'I must ask you a question,' said the beard. 'We shall be most interested in your reply. Listen carefully. It is this: if a man has one thousand three hundred and seventy-six apples in his orchard, and he sells four hundred and ninety-two, how many does he then have remaining?'

I was frankly bemused by this conversational twist. It seemed to lead away from the urgent matter of my welfare. It threatened to distract, posing an unlikely suppositious question. How should I know how many fictional apples this hypothetical man had stored in imaginary barns or warehouses? Should one count wind-falls?

'I cannot say,' I replied fairly, 'does he get a good price?'

They looked to each other. Both nodded. Neither replied to me.

'Very well,' said the beard, having made a note in his pocket-book, 'I shall ask you a simpler question.... It is this. If I have only one hundred and fifty ffenyngs, and I give you seventy-eight, how much money would I then have?'

But I should not accept the gift of money from my rescuer. Especially since he fared so badly in his practice to be staring poverty in the face. I have wealth enough already. I should return his gift with a premium to show my fitting gratitude.

'Five hundred,' I declared promptly.

'Five hundred?, the beard seemed in a tangle. Did he think me mean? I should not wish to seem ungenerous.

'Very well, then, seven hundred and fifty,' I said, 'to show that we are friends'.

'Indeed?' said the beard.

'Yes?' asked his colleague.

'Do you need more? I'm sure you are an adequate doctor. Rest assured, your trade will surely prosper. It is just a matter of gaining your patients' confidence—and never shirking your house-calls.'

'Now I will ask you a question,' said the beard's accomplice. He spoke slowly and gravely. I thought him touched by the sun. 'Which is the odd one out—a cow, a sheep, a pig, a chicken and a bat'?

I thought this offensive—as though they sought to test me. I had already told them I held a doctorate in Natural Science. And any educated man knows the difference between mammal and bird. Nonetheless, I owed them my gratitude, so stuck to my civility.

'The chicken,' I said.

'Would you eat a bat?' asked the beard, smiling

Well, here in Aafryka I had eaten man, lizard, maggot, and beetle. In the East I had tasted snake, dog and sea-slug. Why not a bat, to please them?

'If you offered me some,' I said. 'It is good?'

But they did not reply. Evidently their specialism lay in posing questions. Perhaps the Hippocratic Oath forbids them to answer. Nor did they fulfil their promise of food, thought it was plain, from the loud rumblings of my belly, that a meal would not come amiss. But they persisted with their questions.

'Do you suffer hallucinations?'

Would any sane man enjoy them?

'Do you hear voices in your head?'

Where else?

'How many fingers are there, here?'

'How many toes do I have?'

More than I. Why draw attention to a man's disability?

'How many do you have?'

Five.

'What is your name?'

Friedii: Count: and Doctor Baa MindeBerg.

'Do you have pains in your body?'

When he whines, I try not to listen.

'Do you know why we come?'

To rescue me.

'Will you come with us?'

I have no greater wish. Let us make an escape.

And so we did. I walked out between my new-found comrades. The bearded one threw his coat over my shoulders, as protection, holding me by the shoulders like the warmest and oldest of friends. We descended the tight, tortuous path.

And though I saw them peek out at us, awed and cowed in their hiding places, the savages let us pass out through their parts unhindered.

Coloral Hydrate

Sick, it seems, I lie in an isolation hospital. My mind and body are heavy. It is laborious to write or think. It is a debilitating malaise. They dose me with the medicine of Coloral Hydrate (I recognise its fishy smell). It seems to slow my thought.

Soup cold. Attendant surly and uncooperative. He claims there is no brandy.

Woke and rose. Walked one hundred and fifty times around the perimeter of my chamber. Retire again to bed. Rose, ate lunch. Attendant says brandy unavailable. Ate cold supper. Retired early to bed. Slept. Dreamed much.

Days pass. Can find little recollection of voyage home. Resolved to venture no more to Aafryka for many years at least.

Jaspaa, the attendant, says as with brandy so with vodka. It is not to be had. Hospital does not admit it. Explained to him its medicinal benefits. Yet he refuses to listen or learn. Have no money to coax his cooperation or interest. He spies on me through circular hole in my locked door. It is he, not I, that holds the key.

Have made contact with neighbour, tapping through wall, employing the binary code of Mr Morse.

'I Baa MindeBerg. Who you?'

'zxgheyt'.

131

'Cannot comprehend. You using Vronskii analogue? Deploy orthodox Morse. Which your favourite work of Goethe? Any Vodka?'

'wwqqtydr'

'Repeat.'

'Iwi lliki llyo urchi ldre nwi thde ath.'

He uses an obscure code or arcane tongue. It is quite unsatisfactory. I shall not try to converse with him again.

No answer when I tap on other wall, except echo of distant howls. Return to bed. Sleep. Dinner—stew—cold and clotted.

Jaspaa amazes me. This night he beat me three times at chess, achieving successive victories with greater ease. Evidently he is one of those curious men with but one, singular, grand talent—like that fisherman of Bernfors who can quote the entire works of Bergmaa yet is unable to carry in his head the price of a kilo of cod. Or the elephant at Leipzig zoo which, by tapping his hoof, can give the square or root of a seven-figure number, even without pausing for thought. But in other respects he is like any other elephant, ponderous and preoccupied with vegetables and foliage.

Jaspaa also informs me that I am married. To a Wife. It strikes me as surprising and irregular that he should know more of this matter than I.

I straightways consulted my memory. He is a precise and reliable faculty, holding many details of my affairs. I employ him as archivist and have appointed him official biographer.

'Wife?' I asked, 'Can you advise?'

—Noun: woman acting in specific capacity, as in midwife or fish-wife: also married person of female gender—

'Is much known of her?'

—There is a deal of information—

'Tell me a little. Be concise.'

—She is a mature biped, mother of your children, your partner in life, enthusiast of bonnets and bustles—

'Does she have a personal name?'

—Alyse—

I thought this a very pretty elegant label. 'Does she have a family name?' I asked.

—Baa MindeBerg. It is the same as your own—

This struck me as a wonderfully fortuitous coincidence. I took it as some happy augury that we might be favourably well-suited.

'Is a wife a good and serviceable appliance? Are they much sought and collected?'

—Most men seek but one. Some do without, favouring none. A few men, having mislaid their first, might then procure a second—

'So generally, then, you would commend a wife as a singular and durable item?

—Indeed. Though they are variable in quality—

'And mine?' I asked, eager for more news of this unsuspected asset, 'does she bring credit to the category? Is she a fine exemplar?

—With any wife, there are fine and faulty features. No man accounts his wife perfection—

'Do I detect some diplomacy, some judicious phrasing, to your last retort?' For I can always tell when he seeks to play me false. Nonetheless, he is by and large a conscientious and faithful servile. I try not to irritate him, for fear of losing him from my employ. Without him I should be quite lost—unable to keep appointments, recall my name, speak any language, recollect my favourite colour or recognise my face in a mirror.

—I am but Memory—he replied, weary and peevish— You push me hard. You demand much of me. I do my best. I am the sole remembrancer. If you do not like what I tell you complain to Reason, Sensation or Passion. Theirs is the gossip. They tell me all I know—

'Thank you.' It is wise to be polite to him. I should not wish him to abscond with all my files. There have been moments of tiredness and stress when he has not answered to my calls. He ignores the knock and will not

133

open the library door. 'You are a wonderfully obliging and diligent faculty.'

—The Opossum—Family *Didelphyidae*—are largely arboreal and nocturnal...—he had suddenly grown garrulous, drunk on the dregs of my flattery.—Amongst them we count the Australasian Phalangers and American marsupials...—

'Thank you. That is a rare and important snippet and I have glad that you have shared it with me.' I'd noted his enthusiasm for animals, 'Might we return to the genus "wife"?'

—As I recall, she is not an unpleasant woman. Though her features are not strikingly memorable, I can provide a complete picture. Being busy, she leaves her traces—

'You spoke of some faults?'

—She is flawed by melancholia—

Ah. Poor woman. In her life she must have met some sadness, as I have, too, myself. Life can be spiteful.

—She entertains other men—

Companionship is a wonderful consolation. It can quite cure solitude.

—She kisses them—

'Kisses?'

—A bi-oral phenomenon, restricted to the humanoids—

'Achieving what, exactly?'

—It is a symptom of affection, sometime precursor to sexual congress—

'Sexual congress?'

And he then proceeded to tell me the most extraordinary and unlikely tale.

'Really!' I said, for I was shocked and startled. 'Is this some jape or jest? Are you fibbing?'

—I am not an author of fictions— he observed self-righteously.

'But they do that? With those? There is vasocongestion to the corpus spongiosum, and to the dorsal cylinders of the corpora cavernosa? There is a heavy transudate? Mucoid secretion? An insertion to the ostium vaginae?

Leading to pubococcygeal muscle spasms?'

—Exactly so—

'And people find this satisfactory? No one complains? Is it not very insanitary?'

—Nonetheless persons do it. Often. Frequently in pairs—

'And you say, one does this with a "wife"?'

—Some will do it with none other—He had set me to vigorous thought. I was astounded and intrigued.

'And is there some convention as to time and place—as with dinner, for example, tennis or bathing.'

—Privacy is preferred. The bedroom is favoured—

'I am pleased to hear so.' For in truth it all sounded quite personal and intimate. 'Does it waste much time?'

—It can induce both pleasure and children—

This seemed a curious combination and abundance. 'Tell me more!' And so he did

—The bedroom is favoured, for privacy is preferred—

'I am pleased to hear so.' For it had struck me as a very personal business, 'Does it use much time?'

—It can produce both pleasure and children—

'Tell me more. Remind me of this business of a wife.' For I liked listening to this story.

Reason has been telling me tales. So I have spoken again to Memory to call him to answer the charges.

—You called?—

'That's what I mean to find out.'

—Ah. If you wished I might hum you a tune, I know you are fond of the Kreutzer Sonata. Or I could show you some pictures of Florence or Pisa. Or give you the sniff of ground coffee, as though in your very nostrils—

I knew that he sought to distract me.

'Tell me, Memory, how I know you are there.'

—It is one of those things I remember for you. That I exist. Also my means of work and conditions of service—

'In that case, you might while away the whole day and I should be none the wiser. Unless you whistled to signal your presence.'

—But it would not happen—he stuttered—For I work hard for you—

'And there is another matter. Suppposing I distrust what you tell me?'

—Then you might ask me for a second opinion. To allow me confirm my veracity—.

'Reason warned me as much.'

—He is sly. He speaks well of no one. You should see the nonsense he passes on to me—.

'What if I asked you to remember ill of yourself?'

—I forget—he said—A character cannot be expected to wage a campaign of gossip against his own reputation—

'Where do I go for information?'

—To me. To me—he could not resist the brag. And so I cornered him.

'But you are old and stale. You are out of date. You are an old man, snuffling at the fireside, drivelling of days long gone.'

—History tells us much. Why it was only in '65...—

'But I cut him short: 'What if I want to know of now?'

—I have their records. Each and every now there has been. All except the current issue. I suspect it is unimportant—

'It is the present!' I could not resist a tone of sarcasm.

—Rest assured—he gloated—I shall have it tidy by tomorrow—

'But if I want to know now?'

—We cannot allow ourselves to be distracted by every brief novelty—he observed piously, like a schoolmaster scolding children for watching others at play through the window.

We both fell silent. We had reached an impasse. I could see no escape. He had me strapped.

—Don't alarm yourself—he piped up cheerily—Rest assured. I'll forget the whole conundrum—

But it struck me as a mad house where a man is trapped in the past by his memory and locked in the present by Jaspaa.

'When shall I be released?' I demanded of Jaspaa when he brought my lunch tray. He sat wearily on the corner of my bed and scratched languidly at his ears.

'It is a fine thing that you ask me thus. When a man thinks to the end of his journey, he has already done a deal of the distance. It is a good sign to ask that question. Eat your fish. Fish strengthens a man's mind. We know a man is better when he starts to wolf his fish. And when he shows a healthy interest in the weather.'

'It is cloudy today,' I observed between mouthfuls.

'Of course . . .' he eyed me keenly, 'some seek to deceive. They speak of the weather, but they have no interest or sincerity. We must sort out those from the true believers.'

'I do hope it will be a brighter day tomorrow,' I said with cheery enthusiasm. 'My fish is very tasty.'

He gazed keenly, deep into the folds of my face, but without any show of warmth.

'I thought of my wife today. My memory reminded me.'

'Ah,' said Jaspaa, showing his face knew an innocent smile 'A wife is a fine thing.'

'She is a woman. Her name is Alyse. She collects hats. We have sexual congress. There is a deal of vasocongestion and various secretions. It is quite diverting. If a man seeks recreation, it is better than billiards or whist.'

'You wish to see her?' His face was stretched by the smug smirk he wore at chess when capturing one of my major pieces.

'Indeed. I should like to meet her. I'm told she's not unpleasant.'

'And you would behave yourself?'

'Most certainly.' I smiled and subdued a welling anger. But it struck me as a lunatic hospital where a man of grand family, and eminent biologist, need defend himself against the unsubstantiated slurs of a peasant, and must prattle about the weather, merely to enjoy a few pubococcygeal spasms in the company of his wife.

'Look!' I announced with a radiant smile, 'the glowing face of our friend the sun pokes his happy face around the glum clouds.'

137

Jaspaa rose bearing my plate on which lay the bare shining white skeleton of the hake. I had eaten even the head and fins. 'I shall tell the doctors how you eat and speak.' he said, patting my shoulders.

This evening he returned for our session of chess. I beat him in each of four quick games. Then I let him win the last. For it had occurred to me I needed his help and should show him friendship.

As the bell sounded my bed-time, he slid a silver frame from the pocket of his overall, laying it upright on my table.

'Your wife,' he said. I thought he was teasing. And I knew this could not be her. Then he explained: 'Her pretty face.'

So I took her to bed wth me and examined her forms by the flickering light of the candle stub. She smiled weakly back at me. Hers was the expression of a frightened child by the sea, flinching from the spray, pretending to enjoy the waves. I felt a glow of sad warmth. For I knew I could aid her in her perplex.

Congress?

Sunny but frigid. Easterly wind.

I must write it down quickly, lest he forgets. Mind has Reason to distrust him.

Yet what first? When there is so much of her so good. Her lovely face, those brown tresses, curtain to her amber ears, the gentle lilt of her kindly tones, the beauty spot—snug on her neck, the nobility of her shy manners, the fruity splendours of her hat, the discreet providence of her chest, the dignified excellence of her sadness, belied by the impudent upturn of her nose, those darting, hesitant hazel eyes.

Any perceptive man could have seen that she was nervous. I promptly pounced to set her at ease, shaking her small plump fingers, bowing gallantly, gesturing her to sit.

'It is a great pleasure to meet you, Countess. We are man and wife. I keep your portrait ever at my bedside, and often think of you. You are yet more exquisite than your daguerrotype.'

'Yes, Friedryk.' She smiled wanly.

'There. That's the way.' I smiled solicitously into her shy face, 'We are on Christian name terms already.'

She sat upright, opposite me, her arms stiff to her sides, her gaze flitting across the table top. Though Jaspaa stood at the window pretending to watch through the bars down to the fountain below, I could tell he was listening.

'It is windy today, Alyse,' I observed, 'though the sun beams down upon us.'

'Yes, Friedryk.'

'Do you enjoy the weather. I find it most compelling.'

'Yes Friedryk.' This delicate phrase was to prove a delighting leitmotif in the melody of her sonata.

'There is always something happening with it, providing food for thought and material for substantive debate. When it is not dry, it rains. When it is not cloudy, why then it shines. There are no negative terms with it. Any state can be assigned a positive value.'

'Yes, Friedryk.'

Though no man might call her beautiful, she was possessed of a definite presence. And there was a sadness which coaxed sympathy. It was plain she'd suffered sadness.

—Ask her of Mr Aaskvist—

'No,' I cried, causing her to flinch, clutch at the table and pass a pleading glance to Jaspaa.

'Forgive me. I am sorry,' I said, 'I did not mean to alarm you. Memory tried to prompt me. I have dismissed him. He shall not barge his way into our conversation.'

'Be calm,' warned Jaspaa, eyeing me steadily.

Her left eye was darker than the other, offering a contrast of mocha and umber. I did not think it an imperfection, nor even mention I had noticed.

'You smell well, wife.' And indeed she did. Her confection of citrus and cologne had quite banished the tang of my bedding.

'You are quite as fresh as a lemon.'

She flushed to the compliment.

Her nose would not be documented as either fine or delicate, for there was blunt broadness to a perky snub. But is struck me as an amiable and functional item, such as might feel at home in the nursery and form friendly terms with an aunt. Yet the lips were full and gorged, pouting pink.

'Those are handsome lips.' Again she reddened, fluttering fine lashes and staring downwards. I realised this woman warmed to flattery.

'There is much we might do here,' I filled the pause to ease her embarrassment, 'We could play chess, take a promenade around the room, in whichever direction you chose. Or should you prefer, we could kiss.'

'Might we sit here and talk?' But having said as much she then fell silent.

'I do admire the sculptural exuberance of your hat, Alyse. What are those red balls? Do they signify?'

'They are cherries.'

'Then the larger green spheres are apples?'

'Indeed, Friedryk.'

'It is a striking head piece, Alyse. A veritable cornucopia.' And she smiled at this, at me.

'You should tolerate no criticism of your chest.' I could see the creamy higher slopes heave beneath a floral lace. 'Nature served you a proper portion.'

'Thank you, Friedryk.'

It did occur to me that I was carrying the weight of the conversation. Very well if she were shy. But was I tedious or overbearing?

'Do I bore you, Alyse?'

'No, Friedryk.'

'Good, then. I so wish us to be friends.'

And here I moved her to tears. A trickle descended from each eye, washing winding paths through the powder on her cheeks.

'If you wish, we could engage in sexual congress.'

She shook her head, snuffling, dabbing at her eyes with a wadge of linen.

'Now is not the time or place?' I guessed.

'No,' she sniffed and rubbed away at her nose.

'Anyway,' I said cheerfully, to show I did not care. 'It would embarrass and distress Jaspaa who has no wife of his own.'

—You have a grievance with this woman—

But I ignored his call. I was not prepared for memory to

141

drive a wedge between man and wife. Though we had been talking for but twenty minutes, I felt a profound and tightening warmth.

'I do not suppose you brought any brandy.'

'It is bad for your frail health,' said Jaspaa.

'I brought you some books instead,' said the Countess, 'Of a cheering kind. There are the pastoral poems of Milkmaa, and an account of the celibate lives of the monks of Mount Athos.' Oh, this sad-eyed, doe-eyed woman, so mockingly crowned in her perplexity by the fruity cheeriness of her bonnet. We are snared, she and I, in silken web, woven of filaments of sympathies and desires. It is our fate to be together.

I reach beneath the table that divides our persons. Jaspaa cannot see my hand there, dawdling forward till it clutches her knee to its moist palm and presses, through layers of starched then silken cloths, to the firm heat of her beneath. I touched her there to show her she was liked and wanted, that she should lie by me, complicit in life, conspirator to our love.

She blushes, shy girl. I push my hand further, till the crook of my elbow is hard against the table. My fingers slither along her thigh, then betwixt to the inner slopes which wobble their ripe plumpness. And though she springs closed her legs, straining together, I force down my hand between them, clamping it in her warmth.

'There is more to this than molecules or magnetism.'

'Yes, Friedryk?' She looks anxious, still perplexed.

'For the physicists cannot account it,' I explained.

There are things unseen, immaterial, invisible, intangible; forces that Science cannot allow; a mystical abundance. And though man cannot explain them, nor scholars document them in their monographs, yet they will not go away. Faith, affection or her mother love. Let molecules be hugged in their bonds, to form vulgar dollops, tugged by gravity, oxidised or reduced, refined or alloyed, a man's love and spirit are made of another matter.

'We are more than the composite of our particles, Alyse.'

'Indeed, Friedryk?' She shows skittery eyes, like a frightened heifer.

My hand has located a garter, high on her thigh. Her eyes roll and she looks helplessly to Jaspaa.

'Do not worry, Alyse. You now have me. We are husband and wife.'

For we are held snug in a fit by our love, welded in our union, tied by the pretty, decorative bow of marriage.

A good man knows when matters are correct, when he does right and his interests prosper. So it is with this woman. For when she first came into the room. I was struck by a certainty that some missing portion of me had returned.

'You are not beautiful, Alyse, it is true. But you are not unpretty. It does not concern me that you nose abbreviates to a snub, that your eyes do not match one another, that certain lines to your face disclose experience. For you are more than your matter to me. I love you, wife. We shall not be parted. I shall venture no more to Aafryka.'

And I reached across to clutch her light, limp hand, trembling in my grasp. She felt so small and frail beneath my strength. She had the startled timidity of a small mammal. It was as though a bear had clutched a lamb to hug it to its shaggy chest.

Countess

12th September

So the traveller returns, lover, master, adventurer, like Odysseus, to reclaim all that is his own—wife, servant, home, estate. There is no faithful dog to stir its tail. In its stead there is woolly Benjamyn, monkey, squealing and prancing his delight at the master's return, tumbling somersaults, leaping to catch plums in his mouth, hooting his rapture. Clearly, he has suffered the absence of his hero lord, and chortles welcome to the fruitier.

It was with few regrets I left that hospital, though all had cared for me assiduously, nursed me free of tropical blights, coaxed my return to full vigour. To Jaspaa I spoke my gratitude and donated a fifty-ffenyng note, promising him a pot of tea and civil welcome should he come visit me in town. I urged him to marriage, extolling the sentiment and pleasures that may be secured of a wife. Taking paper and pencil, to prove the point, I drew a credit and debit column, showing how far all costs were outweighed by benefit. At Madame Viisinmaa's a man can pay forty ffenyngs for but a few hours sexual congress with a woman who lacks enthusiasm and cannot play the piano.

Jaspaa was a decent attendant. I shall try remember to post him a volume on meteorology. He has a passion for the weather but his observations are superficial and descriptive, lacking any analytic depth.

I have brought with me the papier-mâché scale models of rhinoceros, hippopotamus, elephant and hydrax, I built to tighten the slack hours of convalescence. They will look well in my study when I have painted them to their proper colours.

There is much to be written of my travels in Aafryka, tales of fortitude, adventure, suffering and defiance; some incidents too pungent for feminine ears; others that might reek of braggartry unless drawn slowly from any unwilling teller and sprinkled by his seasonings of modesty and irony. I have these notes of all that passed. Some time I shall write it out with the perspective of distance. When events loom close there is foreshortening and blur. With the passing of time, a man sees clearer all to the horizon, can assign proportion, view the panorama, distinguish the telling detail.

I have said little to all my friends that visit—Hoosins and two others (whose faces I well remembered but whose names I could not quite recall). They ask solicitously of my health, beam their pleasure at my return, staying but briefly, awkward and hesitant in the company of their sentiments.

Pastor Briegman called also and greeted me as friend. I felt this a shallow pretence but listened politely enough to his discourse—on health and illness, Christ and the Father, mystery and Providence. To pass the time, I counted and ordered the fallacies of his commentary—tautology, teleology, ad hoc supposition, post hoc assertion, shifting definitions, untested assumption of agreement, seeking proof in anecdote. I could continue.

And he values all this above physics? I did not show him the flaws of his position. He will find out in his own time. We learn at our own pace and cannot be rushed faster. Yet it strikes me as a deranged world in which a community supports a slow mind to preach to them his primitivism. So much do we pay him, he can afford to buy ostentatious clothes. He arrived wearing a new woollen overcoat with two rows of gilt buttons. I have wealth enough, but were I poor in this parish I should resent donating to a dandy whilst I patched and darned.

Soon we may have an end to his nonsense. All that is required is for some enterprising scientist to conduct a thorough statistical test of the efficacy of prayer—by comparing the wealth and health of atheists and believers, perhaps, comparing their life expectancies, or measuring the abundance of similar crops grown with and without a pastor's blessing. Then we might call an end to hex and spell, disband the church, and find gainful employ for the clergy. But I did not tell this to Briegman for fear of offending Alyse.

The house has fallen to some disrepair in my absence; the cellars stripped of all wines and spirits. Superficial redecoration cannot conceal fire damage to the hall. The piano is disembowelled, its strings cut and curled upon themselves, the keys crushed by some enraged hand. Rough brick walls have been laid on the upper floor, sealing my room from my mistress wife's. I shall have them torn down, else they thwart our conjugal congress.

'I do not blame you Alyse. The burdens of managing a house have lain too heavy on your frail shoulders. All shall be repaired. Now your man is returned to you.'

We have a most pretty maid, but timorous as a dormouse (*Glis Glis*). There's a twitch to her cheeks, mad skitter to her sharp bright eyes, tremble to her tones.

'What is your name, child?'

'Sir?' She twists and rubs her hands as though lathering them at the sink.

'What shall I call you?'

'Florynse, sir.'

'It is a pretty name, Florynse, and a very pretty face.' She jerks and shakes like a trapped fawn. 'Don't be frightened, child. I shall not harm you.'

And she is very charming in her quivering fright. Time will surely tame her. She will gain many admirers with her lustrous gold hair, deep blue eyes, pale complexion, slender yet ample frame, beauty spot nestling by her nose, pert full lips, fluttery lashes and flaring nostrils. Were I not married to a fine and attractive woman, I should be most struck by the beauties of this girl, with her flushed cheeks, firm calves to elegant ankles, delicate coral ears.

'Show me your ears, Florynse.'

'Sir?' She flushes deeper, as if I had made some improper proposal. Whereas ears, I think it commonly known, lie out brazen in the public domain.

'Your ear lobes, girl. I wish to gaze into their recesses.' For I have resolved to place on proper scientific basis the analysis of the ear, chart its characteristic geographies, detail and name its parts, then ascertain the range of personal variations. For, furtive in its folds and flaps, lies the key to identity and character. Each and every soul discloses a unique pink labyrinth. To commence this project, I shall take a plaster cast of every ear in the household.

Florynse stands a good metre from me and bends her head to display the part. I see the taut tendons of her neck, the pulse to her jugular, and catch a faint milky perfume of her skin.

'Closer, girl, closer. If I am to examine you properly.' And she shuffles sideways, closer by the breadth of a finger. Her shakes increase and she blushes deeper. It feels as though I am the slaughterer, tugging the cow by the nose to the charnel house.

I resolve to persevere with her and storm these coy barriers. There is no call for such timidity. It quite seals her from society. Master and servant are placed apart by class and station. Yet though they travel by separate carriages, paying their different fares, to their proper destinations, they can pause to smile on the platform and bid each other 'good-day'.

If I cast her ears the first—and there is much to reward close scrutiny—we may proceed to familiarity and nurse the bud of friendliness.

The sounding of the dinner gong interrupted my inspections of the inner wrinkles of her ear. Yet not before I have noted a significant extension to her *Lobe Sinistra*, a cartilaginous excess to the *Canal Minora*, and occlusion to the *Peninsular MindeBerg*.

To mark my return, Berthe the cook prepared us a feast. To start our lunch there was steaming fish soup, flavoured with dill, floating rice dumplings. Yes. I was distressed then to sample the contents of my glass.

'What is this, Alyse?' I referred her to the pallid, lukewarm fluid.

'It is water, Friedryk. Would you prefer milk?'

'If I were a calf, Alyse, I should wish for nothing more. But as I am a gentleman. I shall drink vodka or some wines.' I reminded her of the strong preference of my gender, but disclosed no loss of temper.

'I do not enjoy alcoholic beverages,' she said piously, 'And the doctors advise you against them.'

'It is celebration. Further, it is my home, in which I am master. If I took full heed of doctors, I should spend my days asleep, and wake only to sip sulphur water and wrap myself with poultices. It is in the interests of doctors to cast the world as sick. A man needs a larder, not a pharmacy; a purpose not a diagnosis.'

There then followed an unfortunate altercation. Alyse claiming there was no wine in the house, I gave Florynse a twenty-ffenyng note to go procure some of the merchant. One half bottle was then found. I protested this too poor and too little. Two full bottles were then quickly located behind the locked door of a cabinet. I acquiesced to this unsatisfactory compromise, enabling us to end the petty squabble, return to the dining room, resume our chairs and lunch. There then followed a large cod, baked in flaked pastry; broiled duck with gooseberry sauce; hare stewed in mustard gravy, with mashed turnip; pear tart with sour cream; cheeses and melange of fruit.

'Alyse, do you remember that facetious young man with a stammer who used to call of an afternoon and eat all our cakes?'

'Mr Aaskvist?'

'I never liked him, Alyse.'

148

'No, Friedryk.'

'It occurred to me then, as it strikes me now, that you might find better companionship with a matron of your age and interests.'

'Yes Friedryk?'

I was relieved to have told her my feelings. Honest communion is bed-rock to a marriage.

The lunch and occasion would have all proved quite excellent—but for initial discord over wine, the deficit of a brandy to complete the meal, and the unfortunate table-manners of my wife. Her style in eating is neither elegant nor silent. The soup she slurped to her mouth, then swilled it around the cavity. A long smear formed on her upper lip. This she erased, not with a napkin, but by licking away with a curled extrusion of tongue. Her subsequent mastications were gross and lazy. One hears gulps and the loud transport of fluids. I decided that the first day of our reunion was not the fitting time to tax her on these sloppy foibles. Yet she must be instructed to chew quietly and tidily before we entertain decent company again.

—You eat people—

Pardon?

I removed my shoes to lie upon the sofa, to ventilate my feet, to ruminate and digest. A man's thoughts turned to the imminent congress with his wife, and to the trials of his travels in Aafryka. That dark continent has taken its heavy toll of me. A man must lead and chart the lands for those that follow. But the costs have been high. For I lost there two fine friends, prime blooms of our nation's youth, and shed a thoroughly sound foot, and had those tropics assault my vigours with their mean contagions.

My children flourish, bless them, and are full of childish thoughts and energies. If I can find any fault with them, it is that they do not think fully before they talk. I should have liked to spend more time with them. But there was the prospect of this urgent business with my wife.

A man has so much to accomplish. I must walk the park; talk with Hoosins and my other friends; procure some

149

plaster, to cast some ears; lodge with the Institute a memorandum of my recent travels; feed Benjamyn; instruct the servants; make happier my wife; discipline my memory; purchase another volume for my journal; lay in some brandy; engage myself in sexual congress (relying upon recollection to nudge my hand).

And so I have lain down with this woman, despite her kindly protestations for my welfare that I should rest alone and recoup my best energies. She is pretty enough to please a man. Her frame is strong and sound. All wrinkles and stretches to her surfaces are the consequence of child-brearing and entirely excusable for a mother of so many children. She has some pleasant smells to her. If she is plumper than when we first wed, I should still not call her fat—not for her age. It is a comfortable chest she has to her.

So we sealed our bond anew. I had vigorous spasms and Alyse was content enough. Yet although it was all quite satisfactory, I had some presentiment, as sleep tugged at me, that some ingredient was missing of our congress. But I do not blame her. She is willing enough, in her stiff, quiet way, and offers what she has to give. Only I wish she did not weep so, quite moistening our pillows, wallowing in her melancholy, clutching a man by his sympathies, detaining him from his rest and refuge in sleep.

Baa.